Winter Rogue

A Rogues & Gentlemen Novel

By Emma V. Leech

****

Published By: Emma V. Leech.

Copyright (c) Emma V. Leech 2024

Editing Services: Magpie Literary Services

Cover Art: Victoria Cooper

ISBN: 978-2-492133-58-9

Table of Contents

Prologue

September 1801.

They were looking at him. Not an unusual state of affairs for fifteen-year-old Justin Langley, Viscount Carrington. His father, the Earl of Rutherford was notorious among the nobility. Charming, charismatic, and wicked, he was everything Justin aspired to be, and he had always emulated him, hoping the man would notice his son was the kind of fellow he could be proud of. Extraordinarily, that had finally happened this past summer, and Justin was still living in the glory of those weeks with his extravagant sire. Yet at this moment, the shine seemed to have worn off, for the normal combination of admiration and fear that surrounded Justin as he moved among his fellow pupils was lacking. A chill of foreboding skittered over his skin like rodent feet. When he walked into the school hall, everyone's attention always turned his way, the little rats keeping their eyes down and his friends—and those desperate to attain that heady position— jostling for his attention. He looked back at the rats. The quality of their gaze had changed. This was different. This was new, and he didn't like it.

"What the devil are you staring at?" he demanded of a spotty youth in the year below him. Instead of spluttering an apology and fleeing, the boy glanced at his friends and smothered a laugh.

Justin lunged, grasping the lad by his neckcloth, intent on discovering what the bloody hell was going on.

"Carrington!"

Justin froze as the headmaster's voice boomed through the hall. He heard the collective sharp intake of breath as the boys stilled, waiting for what happened next.

In ordinary circumstances, Justin would not have been worried. Bullying was rife in the school, and the teachers encouraged it, believing it bred leadership, that the strongest would rise to the top. There was some truth to the reasoning but having once been one of the rats he knew it was a vile and bloody path to gain those heights.

"Sir?" he said, releasing his hold on the rat.

"My office."

The headmaster turned and strode out before Justin could reply. The creeping sensation of doom intensified as the boys whispered, turning their backs on Justin. Fury rose inside him. How dare they? How dare they ignore him? Well, they had better be prepared to get their heads stuck down the privy before the day was out. Except then he saw Babbage and Frith, his best friends. They avoided his gaze, their cheeks hot as they left the room, pretending they hadn't seen him. A leaden weight settled in his guts.

With his palms sweating and the feeling of doom intensifying, Justin made his way to the headmaster's office. The door was open, so he walked in and closed it behind him.

"No need to sit down. I'll keep this brief, Rutherford," the headmaster said.

Justin jolted. "Sir, I'm Carrington, my father is—"

"Your father is dead."

The room abruptly tilted sideways, and Justin reached out, grasping the back of the chair. "D-Dead? But… But he can't be, I—"

"Are you calling me a liar?"

The headmaster's gaze was implacable, cold, no trace of sympathy or understanding. Justin was supposed to act like a man, and men did not show their feelings.

"No, sir," he managed, though his guts were churning, his skin clammy.

"Your things are being packed for you, and the carriage will arrive within the hour," the headmaster went on.

"I… I must go home for the funeral," Justin said, still reeling, trying to make sense of it all. "How long—"

"You misunderstand, Rutherford. You will not be returning. Your father was bankrupt and put a period to his life, leaving debts he could not pay. It is all very distasteful and not the kind of thing with which we wish our school to be associated. There is also the little matter of the last three terms which have not been paid."

He was going to be sick. Justin clung to the chair tighter, his knuckles white on the polished wood. It was a nightmare, that was all. Not real. It couldn't be real. Pa couldn't be dead. He'd only just got to know him. They were pals. Pa had said so.

For the first fourteen years of Justin's life, he'd been uncertain his father was more than vaguely aware he had a son. He got presents for birthdays and Christmas, which he suspected his father's secretary bought for him. A hastily scrawled note, only a couple of brief lines congratulating him on being alive for another year, usually accompanied them. Though he had done everything he could think of to gain his father's attention, it had never come. At school he had run a gambling racket, smuggled in booze for secret parties, and generally been considered the king of his own little empire. Yet his father's exploits were far more scandalous, and he was rarely out of the newspapers, so no matter how wild Justin was, he could never quite live up to his sire's wicked reputation.

Then this summer he'd come home from school for the holidays as he always did, expecting to find the usual staff but be otherwise alone. His mother had died before he'd had time to gain any memories of her, so usually it was just him and the staff. But on his first morning home, Justin had come down to breakfast, and there was his father, larger than life and far more fascinating.

Close your mouth boy, you look like a carp, were the first words Justin ever remembered hearing his father speak. Yet, for that glorious summer, he and his pa *had* talked and had spent near every minute together. He'd discovered his father was funny and irreverent, witty, and everything a boy wished his pa to be. The Earl of Rutherford was handsome, with laughing blue eyes, a shock of wheat-coloured hair, and a wicked smile that invited one to share in his devilry. He was a fine shot, could ride better than anyone Justin had ever seen, drank deep without ever seeming to be drunk, and could play every game of chance and win, every time. He'd also taught Justin to cheat, how to fight dirty when losing wasn't an option, and all the foulest swear words in the English language. Hero worship hardly covered what Justin had felt during those magical weeks. Admiring his father from afar had been one thing, having basked in his attention for the whole summer had changed his life. He'd hated to go back to school, and he'd known his father felt the same.

All good things come to an end, Pa had said with a shrug, but there was no sparkle in his eyes, no wicked smile. *Good luck, son. I pray you do better than I did.*

Justin had assumed he'd meant 'do better at school,' for his father had admitted to never having been much of a one for books and learning. Now, just two weeks later, the words had an altogether different meaning.

"Well, Rutherford, don't stand their gawping. Run along now, you'll have things to attend to," the headmaster said.

Justin stared at him dumbly. His world, the one that had seemed so full of hope for the first time in his entire, lonely life, had just imploded.

The headmaster gazed down at him and sighed. "Buck up, boy. You are now the Earl of Rutherford and you've a choice. You can follow in your father's dishonourable footsteps, or you can be a better man than he and put the shame he's brought down on you in the ground with him. It will take time and a good deal of effort, but you might do it if you try hard enough."

Fury burned in Justin's heart as he stared at the headmaster, a dull, bull-headed man without an iota of wit or charm.

"There *is* no better man," Justin said, his hands clenched into fists. "There never could be."

With that, he fled, before he disgraced himself by weeping. No one would see that. No one would ever see that he cared, that it hurt more than anything had ever hurt in all his life. And, if his father was a disgrace, the man he'd come to know and love so well, then they could think him a disgrace too. He didn't care.

He would never care what they thought ever again.

Chapter 1

21st October 1820.

It was a fine day, a touch of warmth still lingering in the air, the countryside gilded with the faded glory of the distant summer months and burnished by the afternoon sun, their vivid colours all turned to gold.

Miss Beatrice Huntingdon turned her face up to the sky, closing her eyes for a moment as the horse swayed hypnotically beneath her. She would have preferred a good gallop, but her cousin Dorothy was a timid creature and anything above a brisk trot would scare her half to death. So a sedate walk it was, with a groom in attendance for propriety. They rode through the village of Tenterden, about a mile from her uncle's house. Uncle Charles had become her guardian upon the death of her father eighteen months ago. It had been a year and a half of strife and conflict and had left Beatrice weary beyond belief and sick at heart.

Unlike Dorothy, Bea was not timid. Her father had been an unusual and brilliant man and had believed Bea had a will and mind of her own. Sadly, he'd also had a romantic notion that one's family would always do what was best for one. He had never seen that his brother was not as kind and loving man as he and cared only for the money. Uncle Charles had been jealous of his title and his success, for her father had been a shrewd man and invested wisely, gaining a reputation for having a Midas touch others envied but could not emulate. Well, Charles had the Viscountcy now, and the entailed properties, and Father had left him a tidy sum, but the bulk of his enormous wealth had been left entirely to his only living kin, Bea.

Thinking of Papa made her feel worse than ever and she shook the feeling off as best she could, telling herself not to be such a wet blanket. Papa would have told her off for that. As they rode through the village, Bea looked about her. Tenterden was a prosperous place and busy and Bea enjoyed watching the people as they went about their business. A pretty girl of about Bea's age was laughing and blushing at something a handsome fellow had said. He looked like a blacksmith, and she was carrying a basket of shopping over her arm. The fellow was offering to carry it home for her if Bea's guess was correct. She wondered what their lives were like. Would they fall in love and get married? Perhaps they would live in a dear little cottage and raise their children together. They would laugh and grow fat on the young woman's cooking, and love each other, and their children and grandchildren, as they grew old together.

"What nonsense," she scolded herself. For all she knew, if they married, the handsome blacksmith would beat his wife, and the young woman would regret having ever met him. Perhaps they would not have enough money for food, or for a doctor when their child got sick. Believing others had it better than you did was a dangerous business; her father had taught her that. Everyone had their own troubles, and one ought not to judge or pretend to understand what they could not comprehend until they had lived it themselves.

"What was that, Bea?"

Bea turned, distracted, to discover Dorothy looking at her oddly. Not an unusual occurrence. Belatedly, she realised she had spoken aloud again.

"I beg your pardon, nothing at all. Shall we take a different route home today?" she suggested, for if she must follow the same path again, she might just run mad.

"Oh," Dorothy said, her tone doubtful. "Well, I don't know. Papa wouldn't like it, I think, and—"

"Nonsense," Bea said, knowing her force of will was far stronger than Dorothy's, who could not stand up to anyone. "I'm sure there are other routes that are just as safe, aren't there, Rogers?"

The groom flashed her a swift grin. "Aye, miss. That there are. I know a pretty route that you'll enjoy."

He looked just as relieved as she was, for it must be tedious for the poor man to go plodding about behind them and following the same circuit day in, day out.

Rogers was right, Bea discovered as he led them on a winding trail that brought them to the top of a hill where the countryside spread out before them like a patchwork of green and gold.

"Beautiful," Bea said, drinking in the scenery and taking a deep breath. She felt as if she could breathe for the first time in months up here.

"I'm not sure Papa will approve of us being here," Dorothy said, her pretty face screwed into a little moue of displeasure. "That's Lord Rutherford's estate."

"Aye, Miss Dororthy, but we're not on his land here so there's no harm," Rogers replied placidly.

"The Earl of Rutherford?" Bea said in surprise. "Truly? Good heavens."

She gazed at the handsome red brick house. It was a sprawling Jacobean mansion and looked romantic and beautiful in the golden autumn light. Looking closer, it also looked in desperate need of repair. Ivy scrambled up the walls and over the windows, and the gardens looked to be a tangled wilderness. Yet it was lovely indeed, and strange to think such a beautiful property belonged to such a wicked man.

"Aye, he's there, right enough," Rogers said.

"Is it true what they said about him in the scandal sheets, do you think?" Bea asked him, well aware that she was being dreadfully indelicate, gossiping with a servant. Uncle Charles would throw a fit if he found out. She glanced at Dorothy, who looked more disapproving than ever but said nothing, for she surely wished to hear what Rogers said just as much as Bea did.

"Seems so, Miss Huntingdon. He arrived at Chalfont House last month. Up the River Tick without a paddle, so I hear, just like his father before him. Bad blood, I suppose. This time he was shot in the shoulder, by all accounts. In a bad way, too. Infected. I heard he was at death's door, though you know what people are for gossip."

"The poor man," Bea said with a frown.

"Poor man!" Dorothy practically shrieked, gazing at Bea as though she'd said something blasphemous. "Bea, how can you say so? He's a terrible rogue, utterly dishonourable. He's been accused of everything short of murder, and this time he admitted to having an affair with Mrs Jenkins… in front of her *husband!* In public, no less. No wonder Mr Jenkins called him out. *He's* the only 'poor man' in the situation, for he's been made a cuckold and to look like a fool. Their divorce has been the scandal of the century. No, Bea, Lord Rutherford is bad to the core and not someone we should be discussing."

"I beg your pardon, Dorothy," Bea said, sighing inwardly. If only her cousin wasn't such a dreadful prude. "I meant no offence; it is only that such behaviour speaks of a troubled mind and a deeply unhappy man. I feel sorry for him, is all."

"Then you ought to save your pity for someone more deserving of it, like Mr Jenkins," Dorothy snapped. "Come along. We should never have come this way, for we are bound to be late for tea and that will put Papa in a frightful temper."

Privately, Bea thought Uncle Charles did not need a reason to be in a frightful temper, but having already ruffled Dorothy's feathers, she forbore to say so.

Sadly, Dorothy's prediction was true enough and not helped by Bea refusing to hurry downstairs until she was ready. Though by no means vain, she had come to regard her attire as a form of armour. If she looked her best, she felt stronger, and she refused to face a man intent on bullying her without using every weapon at her disposal.

"Lovely, miss," her maid, Rachel, said approvingly. She had been relieved when Bea had finally put aside her mourning blacks for half-mourning. "That silver grey colour goes splendidly with your eyes and your beautiful dark hair. That new bran and egg hair wash is splendid too, is it not? Makes your hair shine like silk, though it's the devil to keep pinned now. Miss Dorothy will be as green as a pea," she added with a smirk.

"Rachel," Bea said, lips twitching despite herself. "How unkind you are."

"Well, 'tis true," Rachel said with a sniff. "She's as envious of you as her father was of his lordship, God rest him."

Bea sighed. She knew she ought not encourage Rachel into speaking so, but she did not have the heart to reprimand her. Besides which, it *was* true. Rachel was perhaps five years older than Bea and had been with her since Bea's eleventh birthday. They had always been close, but since Uncle Charles had taken Bea in, Rachel had become her only confidante and friend. He confined Bea to the house except for a daily ride in company with the groom and Dorothy, and she was allowed no society, unless you counted the men he paraded before her as potential husbands, which Bea did not. She had refused every offer of marriage to date, knowing full well that the weak-willed men her uncle had chosen had been picked for their lack of backbone. Bea knew he had every intention of getting his hands on the money her father had left her, and she had no intention of letting him do it.

Uncle Charles had never met a woman with a will as strong as Bea's and, no matter how he raged, she remained calm and serene. She tried to view his rages as a kind of theatre show, regarding him shouting and banging his fist on the furniture—getting so red in the face she feared for his health—with detached curiosity. This naturally made him wilder than ever, which was a bonus. The truth was, however, that those terrible, violent scenes were wearing on Bea's nerves. The mere thought of enduring another had her temples throbbing but endure it she would. Her father had meant for her to inherit his wealth, to live a full life with a mate of her own choosing. If only he had lived to secure that future for her… but she knew he had done his best with his will, and neither of them had guessed he would be taken so suddenly.

Her throat closed as she thought of him, the pain of regret heavy in her heart, and she shook off the weight of sorrow with difficulty. If she was to face Charles, she needed her wits about her.

Bea made her way slowly down the stair, knowing Uncle Charles would be furious with her for making him wait.

"I beg your pardon, I'm dreadfully tardy today," she said with a smile as she entered the parlour.

Somewhat to her surprise, her uncle wasn't foaming at the mouth and ready to ring a peel over her. Instead, and far more alarming, he looked somewhat uneasy. He seemed to struggle to meet her eyes, and Bea felt a dart of alarm stab her in the chest.

"Think nothing of it, my dear, we know what you ladies are for making yourself beautiful for guests," her uncle said with patently false good cheer, the words putting her all on edge.

Refusing to allow her disquiet to show, Bea belatedly turned her attention to their guest and noted that Dorothy was not in the room. Alarm bells rang.

"Allow me to introduce you," her uncle went on, gesturing for the man to come closer. "Miss Huntingdon, may I present Mr Arnold Runcible? Arnold, my niece, Miss Beatrice Huntingdon."

Bea dipped a curtsey, a sick sensation swirling in her stomach as she took in the gentleman before her. He was of an age with her uncle, perhaps five and sixty, and looked as though every year of that life had been spent in dissipation. His nose was red and bulbous, spidery veins blooming over ruddy cheeks. He smiled at her, showing teeth that were yellowed and rotten—those that remained, at least—and a waft of foul breath drifted towards her.

"Miss Huntingdon, how enchanting to meet you at long last. Your uncle has told me so much about you."

It was all Bea could do not to snatch her hand away as Mr Runcible bowed low and lifted her hand. She could not help the flinch, however, as his wet lips pressed against her fingers. Taking her hand back the moment she could, she surreptitiously wiped it on her gown, determined to wash her hands thoroughly the moment she could do so.

"I'm afraid he has told me nothing of you at all, Mr Runcible," Bea replied, wishing her voice had sounded more tart and less anxious. Still, she had refused every proposal of marriage so far. She could do it again and endure the ranting that would follow. No doubt another proposal was her uncle's plan, though why he believed she would give in to this foul creature when she had refused far less appalling prospects, she had no idea. Indeed, Lord Romsley had been a dear, and terribly handsome… just terribly stupid too, the poor man.

"Ah, and Lord Worth warned me you were a forthright girl, but you don't frighten me, my dear."

His expression roved over her as he spoke and Bea took a step back, disgusted. Spittle collected in the corners of his mouth, and she watched in horrified fascination as one droplet flew off and settled on the lapel of his coat next to what looked like a greasy stain. She swallowed hard as he continued speaking and leering.

"I like a challenge, and you are certainly worth the effort of schooling properly. Quite, quite lovely."

"A challenge, sir? I cannot think under what circumstances you believe I should present one to you," she replied coldly before turning to her uncle, whose temper was rising, judging by the set of his jaw. "Uncle Charles, I seem to be at a disadvantage. Is there something you would like to tell me?"

"Damn you, girl. Mind your manners," he growled, though his voice lacked the anger that would normally accompany such a command.

"I am minding them, sir. Only it appears there is a conversation in progress, and I am the only one who is not taking part in it. I simply ask that you enlighten me," she said, striving to sound as calm as always when her heart was thundering in her chest.

Her uncle shook his head, his expression one of a man forced to endure an unpleasant scene. "Very well, as you will have things your way. Mr Runcible here has asked for your hand in marriage, and I have accepted on your behalf."

Despite having known this was at the heart of it, Bea's stomach dropped. For a moment, terror seized her, and she could barely breathe, let alone think. Finally, her wits returned to her as anger bloomed in her chest. Her father had warned her about giving into her temper but in this instance, she welcomed it, the burn of it giving her strength. She did not show it to her uncle, nor the disgusting Mr Runcible, instead she put up her chin, fighting to appear calm. "Indeed, Uncle. Then I beg your forgiveness for disappointing you both. I shall not be marrying Mr Runcible, not under any circumstances."

"Oh, but I think you will, this time, Beatrice," her uncle replied.

Bea felt suddenly cold, instinct telling her that something was very, very wrong. She did not speak, for fear held her captive. Not that she needed to speak; for her uncle seemed to have decided to get the thing over with and quickly.

"I will be leaving in the morning. Most of the staff have been given paid leave to visit family and Dorothy will accompany me.

Mr Runcible here will be staying. You will be confined to your room, Beatrice. Mr Runcible alone will have the key. You will remain there until Mr Runcible persuades you of the er… ardour of his feelings and you agree to marry him.”

For the first time in her life, Bea feared she would swoon. What her uncle proposed was so sickening, so… so villainous, she could hardly believe it possible. She had known him to be selfish, unkind, and ruthless, but this was immorality of a kind she had not believed could exist in her own kin.

“You would not dare,” she managed, taking a step away from her uncle.

“You’d be surprised what I dare,” he said grimly. “If you had only done as I bid you, we need not have come to this pass, but now I shall have things my way. I’m sorry, my dear, I regret having to force your hand, but I have no more time to waste on making you see sense. I suppose it is not really your fault but that of your fool of a father. I told him no good would come of educating you and treating you like a reasoning creature. If you had only heeded me, you could have been safely married by now. Women have no reason, have no sense of what is good for them.”

“And you think this… this disgusting old man will be good for me?” she demanded in outrage.

“Give me a chance, sweetheart. I’ll grow on you. You’ll see,” Mr Runcible replied amiably, apparently not dismayed in the least by her words.

Even her uncle seemed somewhat disgusted by that idea, his lip curling. Nonetheless he turned his attention back to Bea.

“Mr Runcible and I have an agreement. He gets you and a generous dowry, and I get the rest. What you make of the situation is up to you,” her uncle said with stunning nonchalance. “I suggest you accept it, and quickly.”

Bea stared at him, daring her uncle to avoid her furious gaze. “If my father could see you now, he would be sickened by your betrayal, but you were never the man he was and never will be. You despicable, vile—"

The slap came out of nowhere. Bea stumbled back, clutching her cheek, tears in her eyes despite her best efforts. No one had ever laid a hand on her before and the shock of her uncle inflicting the blow was breathtaking, an undeniable illustration of just how powerless she was.

"Enough of this. Harper!" Her uncle bellowed this last, and Bea turned in dismay to see a burly man with shoulders like an ox come into the room. "Harper here is your guard, Beatrice. He will be outside your room from now on, keeping you safe, and making sure no one gets in unless they are supposed to."

"Like Mr Runcible," she said bitterly, glaring at her uncle with loathing.

"Quite. Well, Harper will see you to your room. Your dinner will be brought up to you this evening and afterwards Mr Runcible will visit you for a little chat. I do hope you will not put up too much of a fight, Beatrice. You will make things quite needlessly unpleasant for yourself."

Bea did not have the fortitude to make a clever retort, nor to appear anything but terrified. She fled the room, uncaring if Harper was following or not. When she got to her bedroom, she slammed the door and scrambled for the key, only to discover it gone. A moment later, she heard the unmistakable snick of the lock turning and knew Harper had indeed locked her in.

"Rachel?" she called, but Rachel was not there.

Had she gone to visit relatives too, believing Bea had agreed to it? No. Not Rachel. She would not leave without saying goodbye. For a moment, Bea gave in to tears and sank to the floor, weeping hysterically, but the reality of her situation was too dangerous to ignore. She must get away and she must do so at once. But no matter where she went, she would be at risk until she was married. Her uncle was her guardian until she married or until she was five and twenty, another three years yet. Though the money was hers and he could not touch it thanks to her father's instructions, neither could she without his signature. Not until she was wed.

Getting out of here was one thing, but she could not live without money, and she had no money if her uncle did not sanction the withdrawal. She was entirely trapped unless she married. There must be a way. There simply *must*.

"Think, Bea, think," she told herself, just as her father would say it when he was impatient with her for not seeing an answer he thought entirely obvious.

She could run to Tenterden and marry the blacksmith, she thought wildly. A man like that would surely leap at the chance of riches beyond his wildest dreams. Yet then she'd be married to a blacksmith, shunned by all his kind and ostracised by her own. No, no, that would not do. She needed someone of her own class, someone as desperate as she was. More than that she needed someone she could get to quickly before her uncle caught up with her.

The answer came to her, so shocking it stole her breath, and yet, why not? If she was to be forced to marry a monster, why not let it be one of her own choosing? Lord Rutherford was at least a young man, even if he was a cheat, a liar, and a libertine. He was desperate for money, according to gossip, and he'd be a fool to turn down her proposal. If Dorothy's words were true, she might be a widow soon enough, in any case. Bea winced at the wickedness of her thoughts, but she was too frightened to be anything but pragmatic. What her life might be like married to such a man was something she dared not consider in too much detail. Imagining her uncle's fury on learning of what she'd done was spur enough for her to put her own fears aside. She might be about to put herself in the hands of a man even worse than Mr Runcible, a man who would squander her fortune and use her no better than Mr Runcible would have, but at least she would have thwarted her uncle and that would have to be solace enough.

For the moment, she had a more immediate problem. She had to get out of the house before her would-be husband came calling.

Chapter 2

21st October 1820.

Bea dressed hurriedly, choosing a warm gown from the collection of mourning blacks she had not long set aside. She hoped it would conceal her in the darkness if she succeeded in getting out of the house. As a girl, she had often climbed out of the window of her bedroom at night, intent on finding glow worms. Papa had known, she was sure, but he seemed to not mind as long as she did not wander far or stay out too long. At her home, there had been a sturdy trellis and the thick branches of a mature wisteria to help her down. Here, the brick wall was smooth, with nothing resembling a handhold, but there was a tree. The branches often scraped against Bea's window at night, sounding horribly like scratching fingers. If she got up onto the ledge, she might step across onto the thicker part of the branch. She thought it would hold her weight, but she was uncertain. The idea of plunging thirty feet to the ground was not a happy one, but the prospect of fighting off the disgusting Mr Runcible was far worse and propelled her to the window the moment she was dressed. If she was lucky, she had perhaps a couple of hours before a servant arrived with her dinner.

She had put on her sturdiest boots, ones suitable for tramping through the countryside in the dark and took malicious satisfaction in stomping hard on the immaculate white paintwork of the windowsill once she had pushed the sash up to the top. Getting herself upright was harder than she imagined, as the sill was narrow and there was little room to manoeuvre. Still, she managed it, scraping her shoulder on the wall at her back, but she was upright, and she hadn't fallen yet. Swallowing, Bea glanced down, which turned out to be a mistake. She had never considered herself afraid of heights, but it appeared she was. At least, she was afraid of falling, which seemed eminently sensible in the circumstances. Sucking in a deep breath, she steadied herself.

"You can do this, Beatrice," she told herself. "You *must* do this," she added, allowing herself to remember the force of her uncle's hand.

The skin was still burning and tender where he had hit her. She recalled too the avaricious look in Mr Runcible's eyes; he would treat her no more gently.

Bea studied the tree for a moment, selected the closest and sturdiest branch, and reached out with her foot, pressing down on it experimentally. It swayed hard as she put her weight upon it and her stomach dropped. However, the branch did not look as if it would break. Reaching out a hand, Bea grasped another tree limb overhead and, throwing caution to the wind, stepped forward. She slipped at once, her foot skidding out from under her. It was the hardest thing not to cry out, but she swallowed her terror, holding on tight to the branch overhead. Thankfully, her foot caught against another branch, stopping her from going any farther. Carefully, she made her way along to where the swaying limb could more easily take her weight and looked for another of like size beneath her. Her progress down was far slower than she would have liked, her skirts catching on every twig and bit of bark, but finally she made it to the lowest branches. It still seemed like a long way down. Glancing around the garden, she checked to see no one was around, but thankfully it grew dark early now and the gardeners had finished for the day. Taking a deep breath, Bea sat down on the branch, wriggled to the very edge, and then let herself drop.

She fell in an ungainly heap, banging her knee and her elbow hard, yet she was on the ground, and she had no broken bones.

"Miss!"

Bea started in terror as the whisper reached her and spun around.

"Rachel!" she exclaimed, overwhelmed with relief as she saw her maid hiding in the shadow of a large tree.

"Hurry, miss, this way," Rachel called, gesturing wildly.

Bea needed no urging and flew towards her.

"I knew you'd climb out if you could, just like when you were a girl," Rachel said as she grasped her hand, tugging her along a path through the garden that led to a gate.

From there they could follow a footpath that would lead them alongside the woods to the village, except Bea had no intention of going to the village. There was no time to talk, and the two women stumbled in the dark, tripping over stones and grabbing hold of each other for stability. When they grew closer to the village, Bea tugged on Rachel's hand, forcing her to a stop.

"There's no time to waste," Rachel urged her. "I couldn't believe my ears when I overheard your uncle, for I'm afraid I listened at the keyhole, miss, but a good thing too, for I've found a young man willing to take us into Maidstone. Then we can get to London and—"

"No." Bea interrupted her, touched that Rachel had taken such a risk and planned it all out, but she knew such a scheme would not work. "Rachel, I'm never going to be safe, not unless I'm married. I've no money unless I'm married. I'll be ruined and destitute before the week is out," she said, praying Rachel would not waste time in arguing, for there *was* no time.

As soon as Uncle Charles discovered her gone, he would set out looking for her. The only blessing was that he'd given most of the staff the week off so they would be unaware of his nefarious plan. He'd be short on help in tracking her down.

"You're not thinking of *marrying* that… that disgusting…" Rachel said in horror.

"Of course not!" Bea said impatiently. "Why on earth do you think I'm running away? I'm going to marry Lord Rutherford."

Rachel gave a startled squeal of horror and Bea clapped a hand over the woman's mouth. "Hush! I've no choice, Rachel. It's him or the blacksmith."

"Blacksmith?" Rachel repeated in confusion. "What—"

"Oh, never mind that. We must get to Chalfont House before anyone discovers us missing."

"But Lord Rutherford, miss," Rachel objected, wringing her hands. "They say he's the wickedest creature, a libertine, and—"

"I have no intention of putting myself entirely in his power, Rachel," Bea told her firmly. "If he wants my money, he's going to have to negotiate. All I need is the protection of his name, then he'll be free to go off and whore his way around the country for all I care."

"Miss!" Rachel said in awed tones, and Bea was uncertain if her candid words shocked or impressed her, not that it mattered.

Bea hesitated, hating to say it but knowing she owed this much to Rachel, for she had not signed up for a situation of the kind they were likely to inhabit in the future.

"Rachel, if you don't wish to come with me, I would understand, you know. I'll write you a wonderful reference and—"

"I'll pretend I didn't hear you say that," Rachel said indignantly, putting up her chin. "As if I'm the sort of weak, lily-livered creature who would abandon you in your hour of need. Not come with you, indeed! What do you take me for?"

Impulsively, Bea threw her arms about the woman's neck and hugged her tightly. "Thank you! Thank you, dear, dear, Rachel."

Rachel snorted. "Just remember that next time I pull your hair. Now then, no more gabbing, we'd best be off to find this Lord Rutherford if your heart is set on it, may God be merciful."

"It is, only…" Bea grew quiet as an idea formed in her head. "Rachel. I have a plan, but it means you must go into the village alone and speak to the man who would take us to Maidstone."

"Oh?" Rachel looked uneasy but said nothing more.

"Tell him to go to Maidstone as planned and, when questioned—for Uncle Charles is bound to ask if anyone took us anywhere—he must admit that he did."

"Put him off the scent, like," Rachel said, brightening.

Bea nodded. "Exactly. You tell the man that if he does what I say, I shall give him a hundred pounds once I am married to Lord Rutherford. Once you've persuaded him, you must come to Chalfont House and find me. Mind no one sees you, though."

"Lud!" Rachel said, eyes wide. "A hundred pounds! I'd carry you to Maidstone on my back for that much."

Bea smiled and squeezed Rachel's arm. "I shall reward you too, Rachel, the moment I can, for your loyalty and bravery. Not that I think that's why you did it," she added hurriedly, seeing the indignant look return to Rachel's eyes.

"Well, that's all right, then… and much appreciated," Rachel said with a nod. "But I don't like the idea of you going to that place alone. For all you know, it's a den of iniquity. It might not be safe. Perhaps you ought to wait for me?"

Bea shook her head. "The longer I am out in the open, the more chance I am discovered. Just hurry, Rachel. Come to me as fast as you can. It will take me some time to find the wretched place in the dark, in any case. Perhaps the man bound for Maidstone could bring you to the house before he leaves if he knows the way. Providing you trust him, that is?"

"Aye, he's a good fellow, I reckon. Romantic. Likes the idea of saving damsels in distress," Rachel said with a smile.

"Then that's the plan," Bea said. "Yes?"

"Yes. In which case, I'd best be off. Good luck to you, miss. You're certain you know how to find the house?"

"Not entirely," Bea admitted. "But I won't fail. There's too much at stake."

❄ ❄ ❄ ❄ ❄

Justin sprawled in a threadbare armchair by the fire. It burned sullenly, as if it resented doing so, occasionally emitting a plume of smoke that made his eyes sting. He reached for the bottle at his elbow, intending to top up his glass, and cursed as he found it empty.

"John!" he bellowed, turning his head towards the door. "John! *John!* Where the devil are you, you lazy—"

"All right, all right, keep your hair on. Bleedin' hell, what's all the shouting about?"

John, a man perhaps seven years Justin's senior, though a foot shorter and another wider, clumped into the room, shirtsleeves rolled to his elbows and his expression a forbidding one.

Justin glowered at his one remaining servant.

"There's no wine," he said succinctly, lifting the bottle by the neck and allowing it to drop to the floor. It smashed on the stone flags with a satisfying splintering of glass.

"Feel better, do you?" John demanded dryly. "But there still ain't no wine and nor likely to be unless you get off your arse end and make something happen."

"No wine?" Justin sat up in his chair as the horrifying words penetrated his skull. He sucked in a breath as pain lanced through his shoulder, a timely reminder of the ignominy of his situation. *"No wine?"* he repeated, just to be certain he'd understood correctly.

"Not a drop," John said, folding his arms.

"Brandy?" he asked with more hope than expectation.

"No, you finished that last night," John said, looking far too satisfied at being the voice of doom.

"Whisky?" Justin asked desperately.

John sighed. "There's a couple of measures left," he admitted grudgingly.

"But that's all?" Justin contemplated enduring his convalescence in this mouldering pile sober, feeling like a yawning chasm of gloom opened beneath his feet. Not that it wasn't there anyway but, once foxed, he could pretend he didn't see it.

"There's half a bottle of sherry," John said with a shrug.

"Sherry?" Justin blanched. *"Sherry?* Good God. Is this what I'm reduced to?"

"It is, so unless you're expecting good fortune to fall into your lap, you'd best think about how you're going to get us out of this little pickle," John said impatiently. "You've already sold anything that weren't nailed down and we've got enough food to last us for two days. Then you're going to have to gnaw the table leg."

"Is there nothing left to sell?" Justin asked desperately.

"Only your soul," John replied dryly.

"There's no value in that poor article," Justin replied with a snort.

"Well, what *are* you going to do?"

Justin sat back in the chair and shrugged, cursing as his shoulder protested the movement. "How the devil do I know? What can I do? Everyone knows I've not a feather to fly with. I have nothing left to bet with. I can hardly get myself invited to a polite card party and believe anyone fool enough to accept a promissory note. I'm *persona non grata* among the *ton* after my little scene and the subsequent fallout. I'd hoped allowing myself to get shot might soften public opinion, but it seems they're only disappointed I'm not dead," he remarked, sounding bored and wryly amused as he always did, though the truth was that he was all at sea.

There had been no cards offering best wishes, no visitors enquiring after his health. Though he had always known it to be true, he was alone, and he had never felt the burden of that loneliness as forcefully as he did at this moment. He was four and thirty years of age and all he had to show for it was the ancient heap around him he'd inherited from his father.

Good luck, son. I pray you do better than I did.

The words echoed in his mind, accompanied by a surge of mingled anger, resentment and sorrow, not to mention a little self-pity. Was his father praying for him now, or burning in the fires of hell for all his many misdeeds? Likely Justin would find out soon enough. It was a wonder he hadn't joined his sire after the duel. Indeed, he had prayed to do so when the torment of infection had him in its hellish embrace. If not for John's stalwart care, he almost certainly would have.

His father had been five and thirty when he'd put a period to his life. One more year than Justin had now. Well, perhaps it would be fitting for him to blow his brains out on the self-same day. He had styled himself in his father's image, had he not? Why not go the whole hog?

"What's for dinner?" he asked, having nothing better to say.

John snorted. "Bread and cheese."

Justin glowered at him. None of this was John's fault. He was the closest thing to a friend Justin had, and yet he hated the man a little for having watched his downfall, day by day, year by year. John had told him repeatedly to change his ways, that he wasn't proving 'nothing to no one,' whatever that meant, but Justin had not heeded him. He'd heeded no one his whole life, never taken the straight path when the crooked one was so much more interesting.

Well, he was the architect of his own misery, so he may as well wallow in it.

"Fine, bread and cheese will be splendid," he said, baring his teeth in an approximation of a smile. "And bring the whisky, too. And the sherry. And I need more wood for the fire and—"

"Aye, I'll stick a broom up my arse and sweep the floor at the same time," John growled, a dangerous note to his voice.

"Well, in that case, do make sure you clean up the mess here," Justin added spitefully, gesturing to the broken bottle.

"Arsehole," John said succinctly, before exiting the room.

"You're a terrible servant," Justin called after him, unable to keep the laughter from his voice.

"Servants get paid," John shouted back.

Justin snorted and sat back in the chair, the smile fading from his face as the reality of his situation bore down upon him. He should not keep John here with him. The man might be an execrable cook and housekeeper, but he was a marvellous valet when he had someone worth valeting, and a good and loyal man. He'd stuck with Justin through thick and thin, since Justin was a little over seventeen years old. He'd been oddly kind, in his gruff, managing way. John deserved better. Justin had told him to go before now, usually whilst in his cups and feeling maudlin, and John always told him to piss off. Perhaps he should try telling him again, whilst sober this time. The idea of being abandoned here caused something inside him to shrivel, and the tiny flame of hope that his life was not yet over fluttered wildly, as if battered by a chill breeze. Yet it would be the honourable thing to do, and, despite appearances, Justin was not entirely without honour. His rules were simply different from those most gentlemen followed.

When Robert Jenkins had faced him, duelling pistol in hand, Justin had not murdered the man as he had longed to do, for the bastard richly deserved it. Instead, he'd deloped. Jenkins had not. Yet Robert Jenkins was the gentleman, embarrassed though he might be by his wife's infidelity. Everyone knew the truth of the man, yet his reputation remained intact, whilst Justin's... Ah well, it had hardly been a thing of beauty even then, blackened and stained beyond redemption.

John returned with the whisky and the sherry and the bread and cheese. They shared it, sitting before the fire, sipping the last of the whisky, which was a long way from the best quality, and savouring it as though it were the finest wine. They ate the bread and cheese and were just debating whether they were desperate enough to start on the sherry when a knock echoed around the empty house.

"What the devil?" Justin said, sitting up straight.

"Probably just something falling off of somewhere," John said with a shrug, and then belched.

Justin tsked. "No, no. I am well acquainted with the sounds the old place makes when a new part of it gives up the battle against gravity, and that was not it. That was a knock. There!" he said, triumphantly. "Another."

"So it was," John agreed with another shrug.

"So? So open the bloody door, you halfwit!" Justin exclaimed crossly. "Perhaps it's someone come to see if I'm still alive."

"So they can remedy the situation?" John suggested as he hauled himself from the chair. "On your head be it, then. Don't come crying to me when you're dead."

Justin opened his mouth to protest the stupidity of that comment but gave up. It would only make John move slower and he was too curious to know who on earth was knocking at his door at— He glanced at the clock and his eyebrows went up. Good lord, it was after midnight.

Suddenly wondering if John was correct and someone had come to finish the job, Justin took hold of the pistol on the table beside him. It was loaded, just in case he ever got up the nerve to follow his father to his destination. He lounged back, apparently at his ease, but with the gun resting in his lap, hidden from view from anyone entering the room by the arm of the chair.

He heard John's deep voice but could not make out the words, nor hear anyone reply. When John next burst into the room, his face was the picture of astonishment.

"It's… It's a woman," he said, sounding breathless with shock.

"It is?" Justin perked up. Perhaps things weren't so bad. "Is it Dolly? Or Betty?" he wondered, remembering the lovely bits of muslin who he'd thought had been rather fond of him.

"It ain't no doxy," John hissed frantically. "It's a lady!"

Justin looked at John, wondering if perhaps the whisky had been too strong for the fellow. John didn't approve of drinking as a rule and rarely indulged.

"Don't be a sapskull. Any woman calling on me, let alone at this hour, is no lady."

"She is. A. Lady," John insisted, gritting the words out. "And you'll treat her as one or I'll toss you out the window and have done."

"All right, all right, keep your hair on," Justin replied, not believing it for a moment but unwilling to upset John, who really might do it in his current mood. "Show her in."

John nodded and hurried out again, returning a moment later and announcing, "Miss Beatrice Huntingdon."

Justin stared, stunned, as he discovered John was not as foolish as he'd believed, for there she stood, a lady of quality, looking at him with horror, just as though she'd trodden in something rotten and slimy. Tickled by the absurdity of the situation, Justin did the only thing he could think of, he laughed.

Chapter 3

"Wherein she who sups with the devil should have a long spoon, and her wits about her."

21st October 1820.

It was worse than she'd thought. The surly servant who'd opened the door to her had gawped as though he'd never seen a lady before, though Bea supposed it was hardly a normal circumstance so perhaps he could be forgiven. The house was appalling. Whilst it might look romantic and beautiful from a distance, upon entering the stench of damp and mildew was overpowering. Cobwebs hung from the ceilings and dust had collected in every corner. As Bea waited in the pitch dark for the servant to enquire if his master was at home—apparently there were no other candles—something scurried over her foot, and she almost changed her mind. Perhaps being destitute in London would not be so bad.

"Don't be a ninny," she scolded herself crossly.

There was nothing here a good many servants and a great deal of money could not remedy and, once she was married, she would have a great deal of money which would hire a good many servants. The house could be fixed. The question was, could she manage its master?

"This way, ma'am," the servant said, reappearing in the hallway.

"Miss Beatrice Huntingdon," she told him. The man's eyes widened, glittering with astonishment in the light of the candle he held.

"Right you are," he said, sounding as if he wasn't certain he believed her. Well, it did seem improbable that she was doing such a thing, even to her.

She followed him down the gloomy corridor to a door at the far end. A faint glow was visible from the open doorway, and she hesitated as the servant announced her. Well, here she was, taking her fate into her own hands. The phrase 'out of the frying pan and into the fire' echoed unpleasantly in her mind, but she took a deep breath and entered the room and almost ran straight out again.

The man looked every bit the devil she had heard him to be. He lounged in a large wingback chair, apparently at his ease. She thought perhaps his hair was blond, though it was hard to tell by firelight. Certainly, it was a light shade and far longer than was fashionable. The sluggish fire flickered, a few desultory flames casting the man's face into shadow and highlighting his harsh features. She had heard tell of Lord Rutherford's handsome face and form, yet this man was not precisely handsome. At least, he *was*, but that was not the half of it. There was something else, something that made his presence fill the room. *Compelling.* The word forced itself into her mind as she stared at him, into eyes that she could not read but that gazed upon her as if they could decipher her every thought without even trying. Bea swallowed and, despite the bizarre nature of the situation, remembered her manners. She sank into a graceful curtsey.

"My lord," she said politely. "Thank you for seeing me."

Rutherford stared at her for a moment and then threw back his head and laughed.

Bea glanced at the servant, who crossed his massive arms and rolled his eyes heavenwards.

"My lord? Are… Are you quite well?" she asked, wondering if perhaps he was not entirely sane. It would hardly be surprising after the life he'd led. Perhaps he was poxed, she thought uncomfortably. That would not be a pleasant circumstance.

Rutherford wiped his eyes on his sleeve and sat up… and only then did she see the pistol in his hand. Giving a gasp of alarm, Bea turned and would have fled, but the servant caught hold of her arm. She screamed, and the man flinched, releasing her at once.

"Miss Huntingdon!"

She hesitated, turning once more at the sound of a voice that was at once deep and cultured and sounded remarkably sane. She saw his lordship had got to his feet and set the gun down. He held out his hands to her, showing his apparent harmlessness. Bea almost snorted; she had never seen a man less likely to be described as *harmless*.

"I beg your pardon for startling you," Lord Rutherford said apologetically. "I do not often receive visitors here, and after recent events, I suspected the visit might be, er… bad for my health."

"Bad for your health?" she repeated in confusion, her mouth falling open in shock as she took his meaning. "You thought I… I was here to murder you?"

He shrugged, and then winced, his hand going to his shoulder. "It did not seem an entirely unlikely assumption," he replied, a crooked smile tugging at his lips. "However, I am delighted to have been proven wrong in such a charming manner. Won't you please be seated? John, might you be able to bring some tea?"

"Tea?" the big man repeated and then gave a bark of laughter. "No, my lord."

"Ah," Rutherford replied, his expression rueful. "I beg your pardon, miss. You find me in somewhat straightened circumstances. What can we offer the lady, John?" he demanded, an edge to his voice.

The servant shrugged and Bea stared, astonished at the way the man spoke to his master. "There's the sherry, or hot water and honey. Best I can do," he replied.

"Miss Huntingdon?" Rutherford enquired.

Bea started. She felt such a profound sense of unreality she almost believed herself watching some peculiar theatrical. Reminding herself sternly that this was not only real, but her life was at stake, she rallied. "Sherry," she replied firmly, though she had never much liked the drink, she hoped it might give her a little courage.

"Sherry for the lady, John," Rutherford said, before sitting once more. "I beg you will forgive my rudeness, but I have been rather unwell and have not the energy to stand for long."

"It's of no matter, getting shot must take it out of one, I imagine," Bea replied, accepting a small glass of sherry from the servant.

Rutherford's eyes glittered, making her wish she had not been quite so candid. She had not meant to draw attention to his discomfort, but then again it was all over the scandal sheets and hard to miss. There was no point in pretending he was anything other than a rogue.

"You're a plain-speaking chit, I'll give you that," he said dryly, gesturing to his manservant to leave them. "Bold as brass too, to come here at this hour, all alone."

"My maid will be here shortly," Bea said, putting up her chin and wishing fervently that Rachel would arrive that minute. She had taken so long to find the blasted house she'd been certain the maid would be here before she was. She could only imagine Rachel had endured difficulties of her own. "I am no chit, and I am not so much bold as desperate. You surely cannot believe I would be here if I had any other choice."

He gave a bark of laughter at that, his lip curling unpleasantly. "Oh, that much I certainly believe. I am hardly knight in shining armour material, my sweet, so if you're hoping to find one, I suggest you leave before anyone sees you here and you are entirely ruined."

"I am not your 'sweet,' Lord Rutherford," Bea said, fighting to remain calm. "Indeed, I am not sweet at all but—"

"Oh, now I cannot have that," his lordship replied, his voice low and darkly amused. "You are not pretty in the common way, I'll grant you, but quite delicious all the same."

Bea glared at him, and he bared his teeth in return; a grin she supposed, though there seemed little humour in it. "I believe you are purposely trying to put me out of countenance," she said crossly.

He chuckled. "Why, of course I am. I am afraid if you were hoping for a seduction you will have to wait a day or two for, as I mentioned, my energy is—"

"My lord!" Bea exclaimed, surging to her feet. "You do not strike me as a stupid man, merely an indolent and immoral one, so kindly stop playing games. I have a reason for being here and that reason will be of great value to you if you will only sit and listen like a gentleman instead of pretending to flirt and leer at me when you are clearly too ill to do anything other than put me to the blush."

He stared at her whilst the colour in her cheeks burned hot, and then a smile curved over his wicked mouth. He clapped slowly, his glittering eyes fixed on her face, regarding her with approval. "My, my, the chit has spirit. I'm impressed, Miss Huntingdon."

"I am overwhelmed by your approval," Bea retorted and then wished the words unsaid.

She needed this man to marry her and, whilst he was obviously barely a step away from destitution, men could be stubborn devils. She needed to charm him if she was going to get his agreement to her demands.

"I should think you are," he replied, wilfully ignoring her sarcasm. "Are you even out yet?" he added, peering at her.

"I came out three years ago but have been in mourning for my father for the past eighteen months."

Strangely, he stilled at her words, some emotion she could not read flickering in his eyes, there and gone. He watched her closely for a moment before sitting back in his chair. She did not miss the tightening around his mouth at the movement and guessed it had pained him.

"I am sorry for your loss."

Bea was somewhat surprised by his words, soft-spoken and sincere as they sounded.

"Thank you," she replied, fighting a sudden urge to weep. She swallowed hard and put up her chin. "It has been a rather… trying time," she said, her voice quavering with emotion.

Though the urge to cry was hard to fight, she swallowed down the emotion, tucking it away until she was alone. *A trying time.* Her words echoed back to her, such an understatement she almost laughed. She had gone from being happy and safe to finding herself at the mercy of a man good society had shunned for his wickedness.

He remained silent, and his consideration surprised her, giving her time to collect herself before she spoke again. When she did, her voice was steady. She had no other options, so she had resolved to do what she must.

"I have a proposal for you, Lord Rutherford," she said, holding his gaze.

One elegant eyebrow arched. "How intriguing," he murmured, watching her intently.

His attention, focused solely upon her, had an unnerving quality. She instinctively felt it would be difficult to get anything past this man. He was supposed to be a wicked rogue who lived a life of debauchery, but no one ever said he was stupid. Indeed, he was known for being charming, witty and fashionable, an attractive combination that allowed the ton to tolerate him even when he was desperately scandalous. Intelligence glimmered in his eyes, and she knew she must keep her wits about her whilst they bargained, or she would find herself in greater trouble than she was already.

"I require a husband," she said baldly.

His expression would have been amusing if she had not been in such dire straits. She wondered if anyone had ever shocked him before, this jaded man who had spent the better part of his life immersed in depravity.

"If this is some bizarre jest, I do not find it amusing," he replied dryly, any humour or goodwill he had shown suddenly disappearing. He looked at once every bit the devil he was purported to be, his harsh features set in hard lines. Bea shivered.

"It is no jest, but my life. I said I was desperate, did I not?" she replied, trying to keep that same desperation from her voice.

"You did," he admitted, curiosity replacing the displeasure that had chilled her to the bone. "Go on," he added, with a negligent wave of his hand.

"After my father died, I was sent to my uncle, who is also my guardian. My father was a wealthy man, and he left the bulk of his fortune to me. I cannot access that money without my uncle's permission, nor he without mine. However, the money becomes entirely mine on the event of my marriage. My uncle has been trying to force me into marriage in order to get his hands on that money. Until now I have refused, and he has ranted and raged but has done nothing to force my hand."

"But the money would then belong to your husband. He would have no claim on it, so how would that benefit him?" Lord Rutherford asked with interest.

"My uncle is not a good man, my lord. He enjoys wielding power over those weaker than himself. I have come to believe he uses blackmail, too. He chose men he knew he could control. This evening my uncle presented me with my husband-to-be. I was given no choice in the matter. Instead, he dismissed the staff and intended to leave tomorrow morning with his daughter, leaving me in a locked room. He gave that disgusting man the power to keep me there until I consented to be his wife. I do not believe I need to illustrate the methods he intended to use to force my hand," she added, her stomach churning at the memory.

Rutherford had gone very still, though he said nothing.

"Who is your uncle? And who is this delightful bridegroom you have managed to elude?"

"My uncle is Charles Huntingdon, now Viscount Worth, since he inherited my father's title. The vile man he wished me to marry I have never met before but called himself Mr Runcible."

To her surprise, Lord Rutherford surged to his feet. "Arnold Runcible?"

Bea nodded, taken aback by the fury in his voice. He stared at her and then turned to gaze down into the meagre fire. His fists were clenched.

"Y-You know Mr Runcible?" she asked cautiously, wondering at his anger, for surely a man of his appetites and reputation would care little for the way she had been treated.

"We have met," he said darkly. "And now I understand your desperation. How did you manage to escape a locked room?"

"I climbed out of the window," Bea said, putting up her chin.

He turned and stared at her, and Bea felt her colour rise under his scrutiny.

"Well, well, you really are tougher than you look, Miss Huntingdon. I congratulate you on escaping a plot nefarious enough for any Gothic novel. Perhaps you should write one about your adventure. It would be terrific success, especially the part where the plucky heroine throws herself upon the mercy of the wicked libertine."

Bea gasped and then got to her feet, rigid with fury and indignation. "If all you can think to say it to mock me for—"

"Hush, pet," he said gently, reaching out a hand and touching her cheek.

Bea froze, startled into immobility. His fingers were light upon her cheek, a barely there caress that nonetheless she felt all the way to her toes like an electric shock. Her breath hitched, and she took a step back, leaving his hand suspended in midair. Lord Rutherford was staring at his hand with a puzzled expression, and she wondered if he had felt the strange sensation too, but he shook it off and returned his attention to her.

"Forgive me. I was only funning and meant no offense. Truly, I am impressed by your courage, not only in escaping your fate, but in coming to me, of all people. Surely you must fear I will be no better than your Mr Runcible?"

Bea regarded him warily, but she felt his words were sincere. Of course, she would be a complete imbecile to trust him an inch, but she was tired and frightened, and he had the means to help her if he chose to do so. She had very little choice remaining.

"I do, but at least the sight of you does not make my flesh creep and my stomach roil," she said frankly.

He laughed at that, a surprisingly bitter sound. "That *is* something," he agreed, a sardonic curl to his lips.

Bea wondered if she'd offended him, but he turned away from her and sat down again, gesturing for her to do likewise.

"So, you are proposing I marry you, give you the protection of my name, and I get all the lovely money."

"No," she said, glaring at him. "And if you think I'm that much of a ninny, you have a good deal to learn about me."

"Oh, I didn't think it," he replied, that mocking smile still firmly in place. "Not for a moment. So, my pet, what do you propose?"

"A marriage of convenience. We will split the money, fifty-fifty, then you will be free to carry on your life as you see fit, and I shall do the same."

"And how do you see fit?" he asked curiously.

Bea shrugged. "I really have not had time to consider," she admitted. "I always assumed I would marry and have a home, a family, but—" She closed her mouth, annoyed at how wistful the words had sounded. There was no point in crying over spilt milk.

There was a pause and then Lord Rutherford spoke again. "You could still have those things."

Bea gaped. "With you?"

Belatedly, she realised how appallingly rude she'd been, though she did not think she could be blamed for her outburst. The idea of Lord Rutherford being a husband and father was beyond ludicrous. He said nothing, his expression unreadable, but she felt suddenly uncomfortable and wished the words unsaid.

"Indeed," he said dryly. "No, Miss Huntingdon, I only meant that you could make Chalfont House your home, and that… you could still have the children you wish for. I would not interfere in the raising of them, of course."

Bea swallowed. Chalfont House was falling down around his ears, and yet she had admired its beauty from afar. She could restore it to what it had once been. It would be a project worthy of her ambition. That she might live here with her children was an idea that made something inside her ache with longing. Whilst she had loved her father dearly, she had always been rather lonely and had longed for siblings. She had always dreamed she would have a large family of her own. Of course, she had also dreamed of having a husband who loved and respected her, but perhaps half a loaf was better than none. To get those children, Lord Rutherford would have to be her husband in truth, however, not just in name only. Her cheeks blazed at the idea of getting into bed with the man she knew to be a rake and a scoundrel, and she dared a glance up at him.

For all his lazy sprawl in the chair opposite, he was watching her intently, like a cat eyeing a mouse from the shadows, waiting for the opportune moment to strike. Bea swallowed.

"For the moment, a marriage in name only is my requirement. Perhaps… Perhaps in the future we might revisit the conversation."

He inclined his head, apparently accepting this. Bea frowned, somewhat disgruntled. She had assumed he might at least try to make it a condition of the marriage. Not that she wanted to be intimate with him, but that a man of his reputation would not try to get her into bed was somewhat lowering. Telling herself to be careful what she wished for, she put her wounded pride away and carried on.

"I will need you to set up a bank account in my name and have papers drawn up that give me the legal right to the money, so that you cannot renege on the agreement once I am your wife," she stated.

"Don't you trust me, pet?" he drawled, stretching his long legs out in front of him.

"No," she replied.

He laughed at that, and it sounded like a genuine laugh. It was a good sound, deep and rumbling, and she could not help but smile in return.

"You can hardly expect me to," she pointed out.

"You would be the biggest fool on earth to do so," he agreed solemnly. "Very well, suppose I agree to your proposal. You tell me your father was wealthy, but I have no figure to justify this claim. Your idea of wealth and mine may not tally."

Bea glared at him. "I do not have the precise figure as my uncle has kept the information from me, but you may call upon Messrs Thornton and Cranbrook, who have always taken care of my father's account, and will continue to do so for me. If you ask for Mr Thornton, he is an old family friend and knows of my circumstances, for I wrote to tell him of my predicament, not that he could help me. To answer your question, however, my father used to keep me appraised of his financial dealings and I often helped him with his accounts. I believe the sum to be in the region of three hundred thousand pounds."

There was a stunned silence. Lord Rutherford stared at her, apparently dumbfounded.

"Three hundred thousand pounds?" he repeated cautiously.

Bea nodded.

"Three hundred *thousand* pounds?" he said again, sounding a little winded.

"Yes, three hundred thousand pounds!" Bea said impatiently, rolling her eyes at him. "I was not exaggerating his wealth, sir. There are other investments I do not altogether understand but I know neither you nor I will be able to touch the money for some years, but I will divide them also fifty-fifty."

He gazed at her, his face entirely blank. Bea wondered if he was breathing.

"John!" Bea almost leapt from her skin as Rutherford bellowed for his servant. He flew from his chair and crossed the room, pulling the door open. *"John!"*

"Christ, where's the fire?" John's voice demanded from the doorway. "I've been trying to keep this interfering—*Oi!* You can't just—"

Bea gave a little cry of relief as Rachel pushed past Lord Rutherford without a by-your-leave and hurried to her. "Miss! Oh, that wretched man would not let me come to you. Are you well? Did he hurt you? He didn't—?"

"I'm quite well, Rachel, calm yourself. Lord Rutherford has treated me perfectly well, considering the hour I burst in upon him."

Rachel gave a sniff, apparently finding this hard to believe. "This place is a disgrace," she said, pulling a face as she looked around the room.

"Hush," Bea said quietly, and crossed the room to where Lord Rutherford was speaking urgently to his servant.

"Bugger me," the man said in awe, turning to stare at Bea in astonishment. He turned back to his master and gave a bark of laughter, slapping Lord Rutherford on the back. The man paled and grabbed at his shoulder. "The luck of the devil, I always said it. Blow me if good fortune didn't land in your lap after all."

Lord Rutherford smiled. "Not quite in my lap, John," he qualified, turning to look at Bea, a devilish glint in his eyes. "But the night is young yet."

Rachel bustled up, inserting herself between Bea and Lord Rutherford. "We'll have none of that talk, my lord," she said, glaring at him. "My young lady is just that, a lady. She's been raised proper and kept safe from the likes of you. I'll not have her—"

"Rachel!" Bea said, tugging at the woman's arm. She was beyond touched that Rachel would defend her so fiercely, but she did not wish for Lord Rutherford to take her maid in dislike and make getting rid of her a part of the bargain. "That will do. Lord Rutherford and I have reached an agreement."

"Oh, aye?" Rachel said sceptically.

"Yes, indeed. Have we not, Lord Rutherford?"

Rutherford turned and regarded her and then stepped closer, holding out his hand to her. Bea hesitated before putting her hand in his. He wore no gloves and warmth seeped through the thin leather of her own, warming her and making her shiver all at once.

"We have, Miss Huntingdon. I shall visit your Mr Thornton to make the arrangements. We shall split your funds, fifty-fifty. I shall put the required amount in a bank account in your name and have papers drawn that make it yours and yours alone, to do with as you wish. You shall have the protection of my name, and my person if the need arises, and make Chalfont your home for as long as you wish. We shall have a marriage in name only." He lowered his voice, holding her gaze as he raised her hand to his mouth and kissed her fingers. "Until such time as you change your mind."

Bea swallowed, suddenly aware of why this man was regarded as such a danger to the female race. The word she had conjured upon first seeing returned to her; he was indeed compelling. She saw now his eyes were dark blue, the colour of a summer sky in the hour before darkness fell. There was nothing soft about him, his face and figure were all hard lines and sharp angles, and he seemed larger than life, full of colour and vibrancy in a room that faded around him until she could see only him.

They shook hands, and Bea knew it was too late to back out, not that she had a choice. The niggling fear that she had made a deal with the devil, and he knew the rules when she did not, was hard to shake off. Still, Bea forced a smile to her lips and nodded.

"A deal, Lord Rutherford, and the sooner you can get the thing done, the better I shall like it."

Chapter 4

"Wherein a wedding, with vows, a ring, and everything… almost."

22nd October 1820.

Bea awoke, fully dressed, on a lumpy bed in a strange room. Groggy with exhaustion as sleep clung to her still, she struggled to a sitting position, momentarily bewildered. The memory of yesterday's drama came back to her in a rush, and she gasped as her heart sped.

Good Lord! Had she really done it? Looking around the room, which was empty save for the bed she sat on, and a vast quantity of dust and cobwebs, it seemed so. She had run away from her uncle and made a deal with Lord Rutherford.

"Lud," she said faintly. She got to her feet, went to the window and looked out, for there were no curtains to draw back. The countryside spread out before her in the autumn sunlight, the vista she had loved at first sight yesterday even lovelier when viewed from the house.

Her bedroom door opened, and Bea swung around, her heart thudding. To her relief, it was Rachel, carrying a basin and a jug of hot water. "Here we are, miss. I'll be up with your breakfast as soon as that big lout comes back from the village. Supposing he does. I gave him some of the pin money you brought with you, like you said to last night, and a list of provisions. Though how we are to make this place habitable is beyond me," she said, giving the room a despairing look.

Bea gave her a wan smile, trying to infuse her words with more confidence than she currently felt. "Once Lord Rutherford has the paperwork in place, we shall be married, and I shall have access to my money. Then we will make this place beautiful again, Rachel. I'll hire staff enough to go through the work so fast it will make your head spin," Bea replied, putting all her effort into sounding positive and excited about that, as much for her own sake as for Rachel's.

"When will the devil be back, then?" Rachel asked sceptically.

"Tonight, I believe. He intends to bring a special licence and a vicar willing to perform the ceremony."

"Oh, miss." Rachel's face crumpled, and she sat on the edge of the bed with such a thud that the frame creaked ominously.

"Rachel? What's wrong?" Bea cried, hurrying to sit beside her, putting her arms about her shoulder.

"This is all wrong," Rachel said, wiping a tear away with the back of her hand. "To see you reduced to throwing yourself away on that… that debauched villain, it's so unfair."

Bea smiled and leaned in, kissing Rachel's cheek. "Don't upset yourself, Rachel. It's not what I hoped for, obviously, but if Lord Rutherford can get the thing done before my uncle finds out, then we shall be safe. I'll have thwarted Uncle Charles, which is no small thing. That alone shall give me solace, and I truly am looking forward to making this place lovely."

"And living here with that… that *devil,"* Rachel said in disgust.

"Oh, no," Bea said blithely. "I'm sure once he has my money, he'll be off back to town to indulge in all the wicked pursuits he loves so much. I doubt we'll see much of each other once he's got funds again."

"That part of the agreement, was it?" Rachel asked, her expression hopeful.

Bea hesitated, a qualm of unease beginning at Rachel's words. She *had* agreed a marriage in name only but made no stipulations about the amount of time they spent in each other's company.

"Why no, I just… well, why would he wish to stay here instead of returning to town?"

Rachel groaned and put her head in her hands. "Oh, Miss Bea. You little goose."

❋ ❋ ❋ ❋ ❋

Bea spent the rest of the day with her nerves all on edge. Every creak of the old house sounded to her like the tread of her uncle's heavy footsteps, come to wrest her away from her safe-*ish* haven; every clatter of pans from the kitchen a knell of doom that had her running to the windows, certain she would see Mr Runcible approaching the front door with an army of footmen at his back.

By mid-afternoon she was beside herself and, despite Rachel having chased her away three times already, she returned to the kitchen, determined to help the woman with her work.

"It ain't fitting," Rachel insisted.

The poor woman had her sleeves rolled to her elbows and was red-faced and perspiring. She had pulled out every cupboard, washed or thrown the contents away and replaced them. The immense oak table had been scrubbed so hard Bea suspected it was an inch thinner that it had been that morning, and Rachel was currently polishing the vast range with a somewhat daunting ferocity.

"But Rachel, there is nothing to do. I cannot spend another hour jumping at shadows and staring out of the window. I shall run mad if you do not give me something to keep me occupied!" Bea protested. "Truly, I cannot—"

"Oh, very well," Rachel said, setting down the pot of blacking and the rag she was holding. "That fellow brought the supplies we asked for and there's a sack of potatoes in the larder there. You can peel some if you're that set on making a spectacle of yourself, but just this once, mind."

"Thank you, Rachel," Bea said meekly, hurrying to the larder. She opened the door and stepped inside the cool, dark room, impressed by the change Rachel had wrought here too. It was not exactly full to bursting but there was food enough for a few weeks now, though the menu would be a good deal simpler than the fare Bea was used to. Finding the sack of potatoes, she took a bowl and filled it with what she thought would be a suitable amount and returned to sit at the kitchen table.

"Peelings in there," Rachel said briskly, setting a bucket on the floor beside her. "That fellow has gone to buy a pig, and we can feed it all the kitchen scraps."

"That fellow has a name, Rachel," Bea said, hiding a smile as Rachel reluctantly handed her a paring knife, as though she was giving scissors into the hands of an infant. "He's called John Smith."

Rachel sniffed. "Hmph," she said, and bustled back to the range.

Bea smiled and picked up the paring knife in one hand, a potato in the other. Biting her lip, she concentrated, never having wielded a knife before, or held a raw potato for that matter. The first strip she peeled off was far too thick. If she kept up like that, there would be no potato left. Frowning, she tried again, doing a little better with the second and third strip. The fourth was going quite well until the potato slipped from her grasp, fell to the floor and rolled across the kitchen to where Rachel knelt.

Rachel regarded the potato and sighed. "P'raps I can find you something else to do."

"No," Bea said stubbornly as she got up and retrieved the potato. "I will master this, see if I don't."

Rolling her eyes, Rachel returned to the range.

An hour later it was gleaming, and Rachel had lit it again. A golden glow suffused the kitchen as the fire took hold and warmth filled the room. The flicker of the lamps made it feel almost cosy, and Bea's nerves settled enough for her to finish the potatoes, shuck a panful of peas and begin on the carrots. It was not a neat job, she admitted, peering again at the oddly shaped lumps of potato in the saucepan, but it was one less Rachel had to do. The carrots were somewhat easier, and she was feeling something approaching satisfaction with her work when the kitchen door swung open.

"What the devil is going on here?"

Bea yelped in surprise at the indignant masculine voice, the knife slipping in her wet hands. It slid sideways, slicing into her left thumb and making her give a little cry of protest.

"Damnation!" The curse made her look up and, before she had time to react, Lord Rutherford hauled her from the bench she sat on and took hold of her hand. He inspected the cut, which was mercifully shallow, and muttered an oath, tugging her over to the water pump. He washed the cut thoroughly before producing a large white handkerchief and wrapping it tightly about the wound. "It's clean," he said tersely, noting her look of disgust. "I just bought it this morning."

At his words, Bea took a moment to look him over, noting he was immaculately turned out. Well, he *had* been busy spending her money.

"Why is my betrothed in the kitchen, toiling like a drudge?" he demanded coldly.

Bea looked up at him, surprised by his annoyance. "What do you care?"

"I'm the Earl of Rutherford," he replied, sounding every bit as arrogant as his title might suggest, his irritation perfectly audible. "Whilst that title might be soiled and tarnished beyond saving, I am not yet sunk so low as to expect my wife to peel potatoes. You're an heiress, for the love of God, what are you playing at?"

"Oh, well, it's all right for you, off in town and spending money that isn't yours yet," Bea shot back, rather irritated herself now. "I've been here twiddling my thumbs and expecting my uncle to come and carry me off at every moment. I needed to do something!"

His expression relaxed somewhat, and he gave a grunt that seemed to express understanding. "Well, I shall keep you busy enough now, my sweet. There are papers for you to sign, and the vicar is here. We'd best avail ourselves of his services as fast as we can, for the poor fellow is quaking in his boots at having been brought to a place of such depravity and sin. Really, he's not got an ounce of the gumption you have, my girl."

Though it was ridiculous, Bea felt a surge of pride at his words. She scolded herself soundly for allowing the man to charm her even a little. The vicar was likely far more sensible than she. Still, Bea allowed her betrothed to bear her off to a room which purported to be his study. The shelves were all but empty and, as Lord Rutherford entered, the lamps he carried illuminated a mouse chewing contentedly on the corner of a large leather-bound ledger.

It fled as they entered, diving into a hole in the wainscotting. Lord Rutherford either did not see or did not deign to remark on the rodent. He reached into his pocket to withdraw a fat parcel of documents and handed them to her, then drew out the chair before the desk and gestured politely for her to take a seat.

"The first is a letter from your Mr Thornton. I had quite a job assuring him I was in earnest, and it was a lucky thing you had already written to him with the details of your predicament, or he would have chased me off like a mongrel dog. I believe he certainly has your interests at heart and was saddened to hear the trials you have endured. However, he seems to think you have made a deal with the devil himself," he added with a mocking smile.

"Have I not?" Bea asked, uncertain if she was jesting or in earnest. So far, he had behaved far better than she had expected of him, having made no move to seduce or importune her, but he did not have her money yet.

He gave a laugh that made the hairs on the back of her neck stand on end. It was a bitter sound and not the least reassuring. "I'm afraid you will have to figure that out for yourself, pet."

"I'm not your pet," she replied, unsettled.

"As you wish, sweet."

Bea scowled at him but forbore to tell him again that she was far from sweet. He could figure that out for himself. She took up the letter from Mr Thornton, but Rutherford spoke again.

"There is one thing, Miss Huntingdon."

"Yes?" She looked up at him and rather wished she had not. A prickle of awareness shivered down her spine as she gazed into his summer-dark eyes. His presence seemed to consume the room, sucking up all the air and shrinking the space around her. Bea's gaze slid down the firm line of his jaw, noting the neatly tied cravat at his throat, and travelled on to his broad shoulders, lovingly encased in dark blue superfine. He did not look like a gentleman, despite the fine attire. He looked like a pirate wearing a gentleman's garb, and the air he had of something dangerous and only half tame made her heart thud wildly in her chest.

He reached for her hand, and she almost snatched it away as his strong fingers curled around hers. Once again, that electric jolt snapped down her arm, stealing her breath. Rutherford frowned, and she thought she heard his breath catch too, but that was mere foolishness.

"I want you to know that, whilst you may have made a deal with the devil, I shall keep to our agreement, and you need never fear me. I may be many things, but I have never forced my attentions on a woman, lightskirt or lady," his voice, pitched low, was intimate but entirely sincere.

"Th-That is reassuring," she admitted, though her voice sounded rather strange to her own ears. To be the focus of his undivided attention was at once nerve-wracking and galvanising and she was not entirely sure how to feel about it.

"I ought to warn you, however, my lady wife, I shall make you demand a real marriage from me before this year is out, my word upon it."

"Indeed, you shall not!" Bea said, snatching her hand away. "And I am not yet your wife."

He grinned at her, a lazy, lopsided smile that she did not doubt had allowed him to get away with murder his entire life. Well, no longer. Not with her, at least. She might not be an experienced woman of the world, but she was not a fool, and getting entangled with this man, even if he was to be her husband, would be the height of lunacy. Bea was an intelligent woman and one who had proven herself to be stronger than her slender frame might suggest. She would not be seduced by a pretty face into believing this man could bring her anything but trouble if she were to put her trust in him. A legal agreement written down in black and white was one thing, trusting him with anything else… out of the question.

"I'll leave you to your papers, then, pet," he said. "Don't tarry too long, we have a wedding night to celebrate, and I should not want to chase down the vicar if he makes good his escape before you're done." Rutherford winked at her as he crossed the room, closing the door behind him.

"Arrogant, self-satisfied oaf," she muttered. From the corner of the room came a shrill squeaking and Bea turned to see the mouse had returned and was chattering crossly. "Quite," she said, assuming the creature was female and lamenting the male of the species.

Shaking her head, she told herself to get a grip before she lost her wits entirely and settled down to read the papers.

❄ ❄ ❄ ❄ ❄

Justin stole one last glance at Miss Huntingdon as she bent her head to read. The words 'arrogant' and 'oaf' drifted to his ears as the door closed and he grinned. She really was splendid. Shaking his head, he wondered what on earth he'd done to deserve such good fortune at the eleventh hour. He was saved. The astonishing sum she brought to their marriage changed everything. Never again would he have to use his wits to gain enough money to eat and pay his bills. Never again would he be forced to pray, sweating through his shirt as a horse he'd put every last penny on galloped around a track. For the first time in his life, he could breathe easy.

One would think, after all his wickedness, that even if the good Lord saw fit to give a despicable sinner a second chance, he would wrap the gift up in a package that would make him suffer a little for his good fortune, but no. Not only was Beatrice as rich as Croesus, but she was a little beauty too. Slender and delicate, he felt certain he could span her waist with his hands and longed to prove the point. Her hair was a rich chestnut brown with glints of gold that caught the light, and her eyes… her eyes, were either green or hazel, or some combination of the two. He was not yet certain, for they seemed to change depending on the light. Whichever it turned out to be, they were wide and lovely and at once innocent and full of spirit, a combination he found deliciously tempting.

He smiled to himself as he made his way back to the parlour, where a fire was blazing for once. Justin moved to stand before it, warming his hands.

"My lord?"

Justin turned, surprised to hear John addressing him so politely. "What happened to 'Oi, you?'" he demanded, quirking one eyebrow.

John grinned at him and shrugged. "Well, I suppose if you're going to start paying me, I'd best be a mite more respectful."

"Stow it," Justin replied amiably. "In company, I would appreciate you treating me with a modicum of respect, but in private nothing need change. You've been a good and loyal friend to me, John. I shan't forget it."

To his amusement, a tinge of colour touched John's ruddy cheeks, and he shifted from foot to foot, looking uncomfortable. "It were all true, then? Her tale of being an heiress? It weren't no trick?"

Justin shook his head, finding John's scepticism perfectly understandable. He'd spent the entire journey to town certain he was on a fool's errand, only to discover the reality was even rosier than Beatrice had painted it.

"It was no trick, John. We are rolling in clover and will be for the rest of our days."

"Bugger me," John said in awed tones.

Justin snorted. "I know. I still can't believe it. Who has such luck? It's impossible, and yet she's real, and my good fortune is wrapped in up in such a delightful parcel too."

John's face darkened, and he frowned at Justin's words. "But it's a marriage in name only, ain't it? That's what she said."

"That's what she said," Justin admitted. "But I intend to charm her into wanting something entirely different. I never thought to marry, John, but I'm an earl after all. I need an heir. I had thought the title would die with me, but… but maybe this is a new beginning."

John was still frowning.

"What?" Justin asked, irritated that the fellow was scowling so.

"She asked for a marriage in name only, and whilst if you intend to keep to your marriage vows, I'd be right happy to see you settled and content, if you think to take up the life you lived before… well, that ain't kind nor proper to a woman whose given you so much, begging your pardon."

"Christ, John, when did you become such a saint?" Justin said tersely. "In the first place, I have no intention of living how I did before, gambling till all hours in the hope of winning enough to see us through another month. There's no need, for one thing. I'm no longer penniless. As for my romantic affairs, I'm tired of jumping from bed to bed. I'm no green boy and the allure of such excess has worn off. In the second, you may remember I'm not exactly welcome in polite society, though I hope in time I may fix that. My lady wife needs to move in proper circles without embarrassment, and that is currently not the case. However, I do not see the need for fidelity, nor can I imagine she would expect it of me. She's no fool. I will be discreet, however, and do nothing to cause her any distress, but this is not a love match, John."

"No, it ain't, not yet, but you wish to charm her into making a real marriage. As you say, she's no fool, and so the only way you'll get that from her if is she trusts you completely, trusts you to be a proper husband to her. If you think she won't know the minute you play her false, then you're a bigger idiot than I reckoned on. I've seen enough women weeping over you and breaking their hearts, and I don't want to see the lady tread in those same footsteps." John's voice was terse now, his heavy arms folded across his chest. "It ain't right."

Justin opened his mouth but a knock at the door forestalled any further discussion. The stern-faced maid, Rachel, opened the door. "Excuse me for the interruption, but the vicar is getting restless. I don't think I can keep him in the kitchen much longer without tying him to a chair."

"I'll see if the lady is ready," Justin said with a nod. "Miss…?"

"Miss Chandler, my lord."

"Miss Chandler, if you would bring the vicar here. John will provide him with a glass of brandy to warm him whilst I fetch Miss Huntingdon. Won't you, John?" Justin replied with a smile.

John grunted and moved to the sideboard, where a fresh bottle of brandy waited to be decanted.

Miss Chandler nodded and hurried from the room and Justin returned to his study to find Beatrice's head still bent over the papers. She was signing her name. He let out a breath, only now realising how anxious he'd been that she might find reason to back out of their agreement.

"All was in order?" he asked as he walked towards the desk.

"It was, thank you, Lord Rutherford," she replied, carefully blotting her signature before she gathered the papers together. "I have written a letter to Mr Thornton, asking him to transfer the funds between us at once. The sooner we can get this place in order, the better."

"It does not seem fair that you spend your portion on the work to my estate," Justin replied, inclined to be generous after everything this woman had given him. He leaned against the desk, looking down at her and admiring the elegant line of her neck as she put the pen and ink back in its proper place.

She shrugged. "It is a beautiful house. I fell in love with it the first time I laid eyes on it, and I wish to see it brought back to its former glory. I also have no desire to live like this for long," she added frankly, gesturing to their dismal surroundings.

He laughed at that and nodded, a surge of pleasure taking him by surprise at discovering his home, shabby as it was, had pleased her. "A fair point, but as we have dealt together so fairly, how about this? I shall cover the cost of all repairs to the land, gardens, and structure of the buildings, roofs and walls and windows, et cetera. You will cover the cost of the interior refurbishments and furniture, for you may have noticed there is barely a chair or bed in the entire place. It will be quite a costly exercise to replace it all, if you are thinking I am being excessively noble."

"I did not think it," she said, studying him candidly as she sat back in the chair. "But that seems an eminently sensible proposal. However, will you not find it a trial to organise such work from town? I would be more than happy to oversee the work and simply send you the bills."

Justin stared at her, frowning. "From town? What do you mean? I have no intention of returning to town."

"Whyever not?" she asked, looking so dismayed he felt a stab of annoyance.

"For one thing, I am not yet entirely recovered from getting shot," he replied, finding his voice sharper than he'd intended it to be. "For another, I am not welcome in society which would make it a very dull sojourn, and besides all that, I live here!"

He pushed away from the desk, raking a hand through his hair, ignoring the fact that he ought not to stand whilst she was sitting. She knew he was a mannerless devil, after all.

"Well, there is no need to fly up into the boughs, my lord," she said, sounding calm, but as he turned to glare at her, he found her green eyes flashing sparks at him. "I only supposed you would want to continue your life of debauchery now you have the funds to do so."

"Perhaps I shall, but for the moment, I wish to remain here and see my house put back together." Justin stared at her, wondering why he felt so… so… what *was* this feeling? He could not be hurt by her words, by her assumption that he would wed her and carry on as though nothing had changed. He'd told John he had no intention of being faithful just moments ago, but that was hardly the same as returning to the life he'd led before. No, that couldn't be it, because that would be preposterous. Yet the odd sensation lingered, making him irritable and out of sorts.

"I see," she said, her dark eyebrows tugging together in a frown.

She rose to her feet and moved to stand before the fire, gazing down at it. He said nothing, aware she was thinking. When she turned, he braced himself, certain he would not like what she said next, and he then wondered why. She was just a little chit of a thing, a young woman with no more experience of the world than a mouse. Why on earth would he trouble himself to worry about what she might say to him? Let her rant and rave if she wished, it was nothing to him.

When she spoke, however, she was entirely calm and composed. "I believe I must make something clear, my lord," she said placidly, her hands clasped demurely in front of her. "We have agreed a marriage in name only, and that is what I wish for. When you told me I might make Chalfont my home, I assumed you meant to allow me to live here alone. I see now that I was wrong, and that perhaps the assumption was unfair. As you stated, this is, after all, your home. That being the case, I believe we must make some rules between us, for I do not wish to spend time in your company. I do not wish to play make-believe that we are anything but what we are. You are a man with worldly tastes I can never understand, nor approve of, and I am certain you consider me a dull little mouse who is of little interest. So, I would like your agreement that we share this house, but not our lives. Perhaps we should divide the property into two, with you taking one side, and I the other."

Justin gaped at her, stunned into silence. How dare she? How dare she think just because they were making this devil's bargain that she could have everything her own way?

"No."

She blinked, colour rising to her cheeks. "I beg your pardon?"

"I said no," he replied coolly.

"I see." She was angry. Though she was outwardly still composed, he could see it in the hectic splotches of colour that stained her neck. "Why not?"

"Because I do not wish to divide up my house and live as strangers. If you are to be my wife, to take my name, then I think it is only right that we know something about each other, that… that we are friends." The words were out before he really thought about what he was saying, before he had the chance to wonder why the devil he wanted that at all. He didn't have friends, and the idea of his wife being one seemed ludicrous. All the same, he refused to take the words back.

"Friends?" She practically spat the word back at him. Her green, no, *hazel* eyes were narrowed with annoyance, her cheeks flushed, and he bit back a smile. His betrothed was particularly alluring when she looked like she wished to skewer him with the fireside poker.

"Yes," he replied, more determined now than ever as he studied this curious creature with interest. "Friends. Is that such an outrageous thing for a husband to ask of his wife?"

"We are not yet wed," she ground out.

"No," he replied, excessively patient now, for he suspected if she felt she was being patronised she'd get angrier still, and the devil in him could not resist playing with fire. "But we shall be any minute now, won't we, my sweet?"

"That depends," she replied darkly. "On whether I change my mind."

"Ah, but that would be such a shame when we have all the papers signed, the special licence, the vicar… a ring."

The word seemed to take the wind from her sails, and she stilled, regarding him suspiciously. "A ring?"

He laughed at that. "Of course, a ring. You think I would wed you and not put a ring on your finger? When I finally have funds enough, I shall buy you a proper wedding gift too. Do you prefer diamonds or emeralds?"

"I want no trinkets and gewgaws from you," she retorted crossly, and he suspected she was more annoyed at having been distracted than anything else.

"I hardly think diamonds can be considered trinkets, but it is of no matter. I shall choose if you will not. I think emeralds, to bring out the green in your eyes. They are green, are they not?" he asked, curious despite himself.

She waved this away. "Never mind my eyes. This is precisely what I mean. I do not want you coming around and trying to make love to me. I have no intention of letting you into my life, certainly not into my bed, and the sooner we establish that fact, the better."

"But what of the family you dreamed of? Do you not wish for a babe to hold in your arms?"

"There are children enough in the world in need of love already," she replied coolly. "If I feel the lack of them, I shall fund an orphanage or a school, or perhaps I shall adopt."

Justin scowled at her, frustrated himself now by her determination to thwart him. "You may do all of those things, but I doubt they will stop you wanting a child of your own, one of your own flesh and blood, and I need an heir."

She snorted, such an unladylike gesture that Justin stared at her. What an odd creature she was. Quite unlike any lady he had ever come across before.

"You mentioned no heir when we first made our bargain, my lord. It is a little late in the day to change the terms of our agreement."

"Why? You're doing it, are you not?" he demanded.

She put up her chin, wrapping her arms about her waist. "I am not. I am simply clarifying the details that were not spelled out clearly enough before."

"As am I," he replied, folding his arms.

Her jaw set as she gazed at him. "Very well," she said, impatient now. "Give me your terms."

Justin thought rapidly, trying to come up with something he could work with, that would be reasonable enough she would have a hard time rejecting it out of hand. "I will not divide my house in two, but I agree to stay out of your way during the day, as far as I am able. I will not avoid you in a corridor if we are passing, for I refuse to hide in my own house. However, if you are in a room alone, I will not seek you out if you do not wish for my company. However, I demand that we take our meals together."

"No. Absolutely not," she said, shaking her head so fiercely her dark curls bounced, and one slid from its mooring.

The thick lock fell, curving around her neck and sliding down, settling upon her breasts, where the shadowy valley between invited a questing tongue or finger. Justin's attention drifted, imagining how silky her hair would feel wrapped around his fingers, or tickling his bare skin. He shook himself and dragged his unwilling gaze away, forcing his mind back to the conversation.

"It is not an unreasonable demand."

"It is when I wish not to see you at all," she shot back.

"What is it you're afraid of, exactly?" he asked, moving closer, watching her intently.

She stiffened as he grew near, and he paused. He wanted to press her, to force her hand a little, but he did not wish to frighten her. In truth, he enjoyed her defiance, the way she was unafraid to cross swords with him. He only wished she did not hold him in such contempt. Not that he blamed her for it, but for the first time in his life he wanted to prove to someone that he was more than a pleasure-loving libertine, that he was… all right, not a *good* man, but not a devil either. It was a strange and intriguing sensation, and he was not ready to give up on it before it had even begun.

"Are you worried you might fall in love with me?" he teased.

Colour flooded her cheeks, and she gasped in shock. Justin stared at her. Had he hit a nerve, or was she simply so disgusted by the idea that it had provoked such a reaction? Whilst his instincts told him it was the former, it seemed so very unlikely that he could not help but think it was wishful thinking. Disgust seemed far more probable.

"Don't be utterly ridiculous," she said but, defensive as it was, her voice was breathless.

Justin considered. If there was the slightest possibility this intriguing creature might really be a wife to him, in all the ways nature and God intended, then he was going to take it. Why it was suddenly so important to him, he did not consider. He had never thought too deeply about his actions. If he wanted something, he went after it. That was all.

"Well, then, I do not see the problem. If you are in no danger of falling for my charms, there is no harm in sharing your meals with me. However, I am not an unreasonable man. I will ask only that we breakfast and share an evening meal together."

She shook her head again, and Justin bit back an exclamation of frustration. "I am an early riser," she said, a triumphant glint in her eyes. "If you rise early enough, I consent to breaking my fast with you. However, I will dine with you only once a week."

"Five times," he countered.

"Certainly not."

"Three times," he said, holding out his hand to her. "Three times a week, and we shall at least be civil to each other. I should like to be your friend, Beatrice, if nothing else. But I shall not force the issue."

She looked at his outstretched hand, and Justin held his breath. With a sigh, she placed her hand in his and once again he felt that strange tingle of connection thrill through him.

"A deal," she said, resigned rather than content, judging by the irritable tone of her voice.

"A deal," he agreed, feeling ridiculously pleased with himself. He told himself severely that he ought not be congratulating himself so hard for having won the ability to get up at some hellish hour of the morning to share breakfast with a woman who despised him on principle, but he was an idiot and so he could not keep the grin from his face.

"Stop that," she said, shaking her head.

"Stop what?" he asked, all innocence.

"Grinning and looking like a schoolboy given the afternoon off lessons. I'm not a fool and I do not fall for such tricks," she told him sternly.

"Yes, Miss Huntingdon," he replied, all mock sincerity.

His lady sighed heavily. "I dread to think how deeply I shall regret this day's work," she muttered, gathering up the papers on the desk and heading for the door.

"Now, now, sweet. Let's not quarrel on our special day," he crooned, hastening to open the door for her.

Beatrice sent him a volcanic look that only made him grin harder as she stalked out into the corridor.

He led her back to the parlour, where the increasingly agitated vicar was waiting for them. The poor man performed the ceremony with such haste he stumbled over the words and practically bounced with impatience when Justin took the time to push the ring onto Beatrice's finger.

The oddest sensation hit him as he pressed the gold band over her knuckle, sliding it home. That band marked her as his wife, as the woman he was bound to, who was bound to him for all · eternity. A new feeling stole over him, one that made him at once restless and oddly peaceful. He belonged somewhere, to someone, and even if that someone did not want him, despised him even, she could not deny that she had chosen him.

Of course, she would have chosen any other man on the planet over him had one been available, but fate had smiled on him for once, and he was the one she had bound herself to. He was her husband, and he had the strangest feeling that this was something he might make a success of, that he might even *wish* to make a success of, if only she would let him.

Chapter 5

"Wherein wedded bliss is… elusive."

23rd October 1820.

"Good morning, my lady."

Bea groaned into her pillow as Rachel's cheerful voice rang out. They had gone to bed late last night, for Lord Rutherford had been in high spirits and insisted they celebrate. As Bea had refused to celebrate alone with him, just in case he forgot it was a marriage of convenience and thought to enact a wedding night, he had invited Rachel and John to celebrate with them. She had to give him that much; he was not the least high in the instep.

It had pleased Bea to have Rachel with her, for she was the closest thing she had to a friend, and the meal Rachel had conjured up had been excellent. The champagne Rutherford provided especially for the occasion had also been quite delicious. So delicious, in fact, that she'd drunk more than she ought and now had a thudding headache. Served her right.

"I've brought your hot water and done what I can to freshen your gown up, but we really must see about ordering you a new wardrobe. It was time anyway, now that you are almost out of mourning."

"What time is it?" Bea grumbled, sitting up in bed and pushing the tangle of her dark hair out of her face.

"Eight o clock."

"Eight!" Bea said in dismay. "Oh, drat and bother!"

She leapt from the bed and hurried to the washstand, shivering on the cold floor as she began her ablutions. Now she'd have to break her fast opposite her husband, curse him. She stilled with the soap in her hands as the flash of gold caught her eye. Through the soap bubbles, her wedding ring glinted, and Bea's throat tightened. Last night ought to have been the happiest day of her life. She ought to have married a man she loved and respected with her friends and family beside her. Instead, she had tied herself forever to a man reviled by society, whom she had only known a matter of hours, and who would no doubt bring her nothing but trouble and embarrassment in the years to come.

Resolutely, she ignored the ring and carried on washing. She would not let him make her miserable. He would not be allowed to make a wreck of her life. It might not be easy, but she would learn to manage him, and to keep him in his place. Then she could carve a life for herself out of her new circumstances. It might not be at all bad, after all. She had freedom, far more freedom than any other woman she had ever known. A home and money of her own to spend as she desired was an unheard-of dream for most ladies of the *ton*, and many of them would have given a good deal to have a life in which their husbands played no part. She was really splendidly fortunate.

She dressed as fast as she could, fidgeted as Rachel did her hair, and then Bea flew down the stairs, hoping against hope that her indolent husband was still abed. Fate was not smiling on her this morning, but the Earl of Rutherford was. He looked up, his wicked grin greeting her as she entered the room.

He set down his knife and fork and rose to his feet. Bea cursed inwardly, wishing he was not such a handsome devil, that his smile was not the kind that made you wish to smile in response, no matter how little he deserved it. He came to meet her, taking her hand and bowing over it, before pressing a gentle kiss to her knuckles.

"Lady wife, how charming you look this morning, and how delightful to have the prospect of sharing the morning with you."

"Breakfast, my lord," she said firmly. "We shall share breakfast. Not the morning."

"Well, there's no rush, is there?" he asked, his blue eyes twinkling merrily.

Bea steeled herself, reminding herself that her husband was at his most dangerous when he was being charming. She did not doubt the number of women who could attest to that fact were legion, and she had no intention of adding to their numbers.

"I find I have little appetite today," she said repressively, comforting herself with the fact it was true. She hated behaving like such a misery though. Lord, she sounded just like her cousin Dorothy. The idea vexed her, and she relented a little. "I suppose I could manage some tea and toast."

"Tea and toast?" Rachel exclaimed, bustling into the room. "Nay, my lady. You know you get crabby late morning if you don't eat a proper meal first thing. Now, I've made porridge, just how you like it, and there're crumpets and jam and I can do you a poached egg should you fancy it."

"Thank you, Rachel," Bea said meekly, determinedly ignoring the smirk on her husband's handsome face. The rat.

"It's a lovely day."

Bea glanced up at Rutherford, who had spoken. His attention was on the thick sirloin he was cutting up and so she replied politely. The weather ought to be a safe enough topic after all.

"Indeed, it is. We have had a fine autumn so far."

He chewed thoughtfully, glancing across the table at her before regarding his plate once more. "I have not dared investigate the gardens since I arrived here. They were lovely when I was a boy, but they've been let go. I wondered if… if you might take a turn about the grounds with me. Just a one off," he added hastily before she had the chance to reject the idea. "I understand we shall not be in each other's company as a rule, but it occurs to me that I would not like to make sweeping changes and discover too late that you hate them."

Bea frowned, seeing the sense in this but disliking the idea of spending more time with him. She stirred the bowl of porridge Rachel had placed before her, taking a spoonful and blowing on it before cautiously raising it to her lips to discover it sweetened with honey but with salt on the top too, just the way she liked it.

"Are you considering significant changes to the garden, then?" she asked.

"Well, perhaps. There's a rose garden, which I thought might be better as a simple lawn, and then the ornamental pond probably ought to be filled in and—"

Bea set down her spoon with a clatter. "Dig up a rose garden?" she exclaimed in outrage. "And fill in an ornamental pond?"

"Well, I have not made any definite plans," he replied, sounding offended.

"Indeed, I should think not! Dig up the rose garden indeed," she said, shaking her head and glaring at him. "Very well. I shall take a turn about the garden with you, and we shall see what needs doing, but I think the most urgent matter is to employ staff. It is all well and good making plans but if there is no one to do the work—"

"I sent John into Tunbridge Wells this morning to go to the servants' registry office and see what he could find."

"Oh." Bea considered this as she picked up her spoon once more. "I dislike procuring servants from such places, for one never knows what one will get, but I suppose, in the circumstances, I can hardly ask my friends for recommendations."

"Do you have friends?" he asked, surprising her.

Bea stiffened, sensing an insult, and then thought about the question. "I thought I did," she said slowly. "I thought I had a great many friends. Yet when my father died and my uncle took me in, no one contacted me to ask if I was well, or if… Well, no one did," she said, resolutely determined not to cry though the familiar pain of rejection was a weight in her chest.

"I find that very hard to believe," he replied, his tone gentle.

Bea glanced at him and then wished she had not. His eyes were soft with understanding. She shook off the warm feeling the look gave her and shrugged. "Well, it's the truth."

"Perhaps, but did you ever consider that your uncle kept such correspondence from you? He wished to isolate you, did he not? If you felt alone and vulnerable, you might be easier to manage."

Bea stared at him, wondering why she had not realised the truth herself. Dorothy had told her stories of how busy her friends were, and how they wished to allow her to grieve in private, knowing how close she had been to her father. She had been so miserable she had taken the words at facc valuc, but perhaps her uncle had put those words in her cousin's mouth. "He kept them from me," she repeated numbly.

Rutherford nodded. "I'm afraid so."

Bea set her spoon down again, her appetite deserting her. "You must think me a fool," she said in disgust.

He laughed at that, making her look sharply up at him. "I think nothing of the sort," he said, looking amused. "You have the wickedest rake in England dancing to your tune, do you not?"

Bea harrumphed, not at all convinced of that, but glad he had not taken the opportunity to mock her. She stared down into her bowl again, wishing she did not feel so very stupid. Any friends she'd had must think *she* had abandoned *them*. "It was not until he presented me with Mr Runcible that I truly understood the depths of my uncle's wickedness and ambition."

"He was your family, you wanted to trust him. You *should* have been able to trust him," he said, a note to his voice that made her look back at him once more.

For a moment she wondered what his family had been like, for surely there was a reason he had turned out the way he had. If he'd had a loving family to guide him, surely he would not have sought to hurt and embarrass them so deeply with the way he'd carried on. His face was impassive, his attention solely on his plate as he made his way through the sirloin.

"Do you have no family living, my lord?"

He shook his head. "Call me Justin," he replied, glancing up and smiling at her. "We are married, are we not, Beatrice?"

Bea frowned. It felt odd, hearing her given name on his lips, giving their conversation an intimacy she did not like. "I mean no offence, but I prefer to keep things formal. I think it is for the best."

"I do not," he said, taking a large bite of sirloin and chewing thoughtfully as he stared back at her. "Beatrice," he added, once he had swallowed the bite.

An irrepressible grin followed her name and Bea's jaw tightened but she held her tongue. She was not about to allow him to see how much he vexed her, for he would only enjoy tormenting her even more. Instead, she turned her attention resolutely to her porridge, finding she was hungry after all. Indeed, she managed the porridge, two crumpets with jam, and two poached eggs, discovering that if she concentrated on eating with enthusiasm, it was easier to avoid conversation. She had the disquieting sense that Rutherford knew exactly what she was doing and found her delightfully entertaining. The idea was a frustrating one, but better than indulging his desire for conversation that would no doubt give him a means to cause her further unease.

After breakfast, Bea donned her cloak and bonnet, drawing on her gloves as she walked to the front door. Rutherford was waiting for her and opened the door for her to walk outside. Bea paused on the threshold, drinking in the fresh air and letting out a breath that clouded around her. It occurred to her in that moment that she had done it. The revolting plans Uncle Charles had made for her had come to nothing, she had thwarted him, beaten him at his own game. Now, she was safe, or at least *safer*, she thought, slanting a glance at her husband, who she did not trust further than she could throw him. Her uncle could not yet have discovered where she had gone, else he would have been pounding on her door. She was not only married but married to such a notorious libertine that the idea he might not have bedded her should scotch any thoughts of having the marriage annulled.

She had won. The idea cheered her immensely.

Rutherford held out his arm for her.

"There's no need for that," Bea said, unsettled by the notion of putting her hand on him, even with layers of linen and wool and leather between her hand and his skin. The man unnerved her more than she liked to admit.

"No need, but is it such an unreasonable demand? I am behaving like a gentleman, am I not?"

"Yes, but you're not one in anything other than name," Bea replied frankly, determined to make him see she would not be charmed. "You can't make a silk purse out of a sow's ear and there's little point in pretending otherwise."

Emotion flashed in his blue eyes, making them look suddenly cold, his expression aloof. "What an elegant turn of phrase you have, wife," he said crisply. "As you wish. The rose garden is this way."

He stalked ahead of her, making her hurry to keep up with his long strides, but better that than some awkward enactment of marital harmony when the whole thing was a sham. For a moment she regretted having spoken quite so harshly. He had been kind enough to her, after all, but instinct told her that any show of weakness, of wavering in her resolve, would be pounced on by such a man. He knew how to make women love him, how to weasel his way into their affections to get what he wanted. Bea had to presume he was an expert at such tactics too, or else how had he come by his reputation?

The weather had been mild so far this year, and Bea was surprised but not astonished to discover some roses still blooming. They were leggy and running wild, weeds choking their roots and prickly brambles weaving among the thorny stems. Getting the beds back in order would be an unenviable task, but not an impossible one.

"Some of them may need replacing, I suppose," she mused, daring to reach over the tangle to draw a blowsy pink bloom towards her. She lifted the flower to her nose and inhaled. "Oh, that's heavenly," she said with a sigh as the decadent, heady perfume filled her senses.

"It was a delightful place when I was a child. I used to come her often, with a book or a sketch pad," Rutherford said, watching her with an oddly intent expression. He laughed at the look on her face. "You might imagine I was depraved even at such a tender age, but I didn't start my career of wickedness as early as all that."

Bea's eyebrows rose, still finding it hard to imagine him as a boy with a book. She supposed if anything she had imagined him as a devotee of hunting and sports, even the kind of boy to pull the wings off butterflies. Perhaps that was unfair. There was certainly gossip enough about his exploits, and telling some poor cuckolded man of his infidelity with his wife in public was hardly a kind thing to do, but she had not heard of him being excessively cruel.

"My mother planted many of these," Rutherford added, gazing at the overgrown mass with a frown. "I used to wonder if she looked down on me while I was here."

"Oh." Bea did not know what to say to that but, before she could think of anything, he gave a mirthless snort and shook his head.

"Foolish, I know. The dead are simply dead and have no care for those they leave behind."

"Do you believe that?" she asked, curious despite herself.

"Certainly," he said, turning away from her. "This way to the ornamental pond."

Bea hurried after him. "I think you are wrong," she said to his back, for the path was too overgrown to allow her to walk beside him, even if she could have kept up. "Since my father died, I have once or twice thought I felt his presence at my side. It… It was comforting."

Rutherford stopped so suddenly she almost ploughed into the back of him.

"A delusion," he said, not unkindly, but with certainty. "If anything lives on past death, then it cares not for those who are left behind. We are forgotten, as we ought to forget them."

"That's not true. I don't believe that!" Bea said angrily, shocked by the sudden flare of fury, but her temper only increased as she discovered hot tears pricking at her eyes.

Rutherford stared at her for a long moment and then let out a breath. "Forgive me, that was a… a callous thing to say. It is only what I believe, and I have no right to convince you of it. I have no desire to destroy such ideas if they comfort you."

Bea blinked hard, wrong-footed by his apology and the apparent sincerity she heard in his words. "Why?" she asked him, hearing the quaver in her voice, and frustrated that he had disturbed her peace so easily but wanting to know why his view was so bleak despite herself. "Why do you believe that?"

Rutherford shrugged. "My mother died when I was a babe, but there is a portrait of her hanging in the salon. I would gaze at it for hours as a child, and I would have given anything, everything, to have felt for a moment that she was standing beside me, that she had not forgotten me. Surely, in those circumstances, a mother would comfort her son? As for my father, he took his own life rather than spend a moment longer in my company and I certainly never felt he stood beside me, guiding me, however badly I might have needed that guidance. Though, knowing my father, he would have set me on precisely the path I took. But perhaps I am simply undeserving of such comfort. Perhaps my mother knew what I would become and turned her back before I could disappoint her. Either way, I decided a long time ago that the dead don't care, not for me, at least." He took a step closer to her and touched her cheek, his gloved finger moving with care. "You, however, were no doubt the centre of your father's universe, so it stands to reason that he watches over you still. I had not considered that."

He turned away and walked on, making Bea feel abruptly shaken and out of sorts. She frowned, forcing herself to follow, though she did not wish to. Just as she had known, spending time in his company was dangerous. She did not wish to think of him as a real person, as someone who had once been a lonely boy desperate for his mother, as a young man who must have wondered why his father ended his life rather than stay with him. She did not wish for him to be anything other than the wicked libertine she could not trust and did not like. If she did not keep him painted in those colours, she might discover something in him to like. She might find something in him to care for. That was the road to misery, and she would not set foot on it.

Thankfully for her peace of mind, he was silent as they traversed the gardens. Bea concentrated on what she could see beneath the disorder, discovering the bones of what had once been a formal garden, beautifully laid out with paths and deep borders, with walls and hedges and places to sit and gaze at the stunning views. Excitement stirred inside her as she imagined what the place could be once again, supposing she could keep a rein on Rutherford's ideas about tearing up rose gardens and filling in the pond.

Except why would he wish to tear up the rose garden when he had spoken about it so fondly? With a curse of frustration, she realised he had tricked her, fooled her into spending this time with him. Were his words about his parents so calculated, too, designed to touch her tender heart and make her soften towards him? *The devil*, she thought angrily.

The ornamental pond was thick with weed and slime, but the large rectangle was elegant, and she could see at once it would be a lovely, tranquil spot to spend time in. Still seething, she walked up to Rutherford, who was staring into the murky water.

"You never had the slightest intention of pulling up the roses, did you? Nor of filling in this pond?"

Rutherford straightened and turned to look at her, a slow smile curving over his wicked mouth. In that moment, he looked every inch the heartless rake he was purported to be. "Ah, but how else to get you to walk in the garden with me?"

Bea glared at him. "Well, you may be certain I shall not fall for such tricks again. Good day to you, my lord," she said, and turned and stalked away.

❄ ❄ ❄ ❄ ❄

Justin watched Bea hurry away from him, head held high. He wondered why he'd done it, why he had not looked rueful and admitted to his trickery in a manner that would just have made her roll her eyes, instead of giving her greater reason to mistrust him and every word he spoke. He could have done it, could have charmed her into forgiving him, but he hadn't.

Cursing, he kicked a stone from the moss-covered path. It slid into the murky water with a disconsolate plop, immediately devoured by thick green weed and drawn out of sight.

"Damned fool," he muttered under his breath.

What did he care if she despised him? It was nothing to him. He had her money now, had the means to return his home to its former glory, had the means to ensure he could walk among the *ton* with his head up if he so wished, despite the fact they loathed him, that most of them would cut him without a second thought. There would always be women hungry enough for his talents, and now for his fortune; females who would flirt and flatter and invite him into their beds. Wasn't that everything he'd wanted? He'd needed a miracle to restore his fortunes, and one had landed in his lap. So what if that miracle had the shape and visage of a fairy queen, intricate and delicate… and dangerous too? She was no pretty face, his wife, no silly child to be moulded and manoeuvred as he desired, despite her youth and inexperience. Innocent she might be, but she was as sharp and cunning as a wild creature, and he did not doubt she would bare her teeth if he pushed too hard.

The thought gave him an oddly restless feeling.

He told himself to forget her. She didn't want him, and he had no desire to spend the time required to woo her to his side. *Assuming he could do it*, a little voice whispered in his ear. Of course he could, he returned, indignant. He'd never failed to seduce his quarry once he'd decided upon whom he desired. But then he had never been attracted to innocence, never found any appeal in those women who knew nothing of passion, nor how to please a man. It seemed to him a very dull way to spend his time, schooling a girl with no experience who would likely weep and demand he marry her the moment it was done. No, thank you very much. Far better a bored wife, or a widow who knew what they were about, knew the risks they took and found the affair even more exciting because of it. So, he'd do well to remember that and give his wife the wide berth she had demanded of him.

With that resolution made, he carried on walking, making mental notes about where the most immediate work would need to be focused. Yet all the while Beatrice's face lingered in the back of his mind, the way tears had sparkled in her eyes when he had suggested she had imagined her father's presence from beyond the grave. She was such a solemn little thing, so weighed down by circumstance, by the need to be self-possessed and brave. What might she have been like if her father had not died, leaving her in the hands of her despicable uncle? For all the dreadful things Justin had done in his life, he could have nothing but contempt for a man who bullied and connived and used force to gain what he wanted. If either her uncle, or the vile Mr Runcible ever put themselves in his path, Justin would take great satisfaction in revenging himself on them on her behalf. Not that she needed his help. She had saved herself, had she not? Bearded the lion in his den and negotiated a deal that got her everything she wanted: his name, his home, and nothing whatsoever to do with him.

He laughed, though it was a bitter sound, and the new delight of spending vast sums of money repairing his home and making it grand again seemed suddenly hollow.

Chapter 6

*"Wherein the dust settles, or billows, depending on your point of
view."*

1ˢᵗ *November 1820.*

"It's a wonder what can be done in little more than a week,"
Rachel said, standing back and admiring their handiwork.

Bea nodded, not beyond giving herself a mental pat on the
back as she regarded her new parlour with approval. Throwing
enormous sums of money and a good many servants at a job did
make things happen at speed. They had turned the house upside
down over the past days, soot and dust invading every room as the
new army of servants got to work. Life had settled itself into a new
routine which had become surprisingly familiar in a short time.
Bea rose early, avoiding Rutherford, broke her fast in blessed
peace in the smallest parlour—which had been the easiest to clean
and furnish as a temporary breakfast room—and then got down to
the business of organising staff, choosing paint colours and
ordering curtains and furniture from the vast array of brochures,
more of which arrived every morning.

The scent of fresh paint still filled the room, sharp and
astringent despite the bowls of potpourri she had set upon side
tables, but the parlour she had chosen as her own private space was
complete. This, the kitchen, and her bedroom she had earmarked as
being the most urgent. She hoped Rutherford had no illusions
about her decorating and furnishing *his* room, for she would not set
foot in that den of iniquity for all the tea in China.

Still, the parlour was a magnificent success. Yes, there were
still gaps that needed furniture, spaces on the walls crying out for
paintings, but those things were in hand, and she did not wish to

rush but to take pleasure in the details. The room looked marvellous, though, painted in shades of green and blue with touches of gold and rich amber in the soft furnishings. The autumn landscape beyond the window contrasted beautifully, highlighting the warmer tones and making her eager to curl up in one of the large, comfortable chairs she had placed by the crackling fire. Soon it would be time to draw the thick damask curtains as the sun set behind the trees and the last of the daylight fled the sky. Bea was looking forward to it, to the sensation of being safe and warm in a room that made you feel cosseted. Though she still lived in a state of nervous excitement awaiting the day her uncle appeared on her doorstep, the knowledge that she was safe now was an extraordinary blessing after so many months of stress.

Bea moved around the room, touching items she had chosen as she went, plumping a lovely velvet cushion, admiring the new mantel clock as it ticked softly and steadily. The chimney had been swept so there was no belching or smoking, and Rutherford had got his workmen to repair the windows after she had written a polite note requesting it done, and handed to Rachel, who gave it to John, and then he to her husband.

She had, miraculously, seen nothing of Rutherford since that day in the garden. Though it was a large house, she had assumed they would run into each other often, but either by luck or design, it had not happened. Neither had he demanded she appear at dinner, as he had insisted upon her agreeing to. Each night she had expected the summons, knowing she could not refuse, for she had given her word, but it had never come. Strangely, despite it being exactly what she had wanted and hoped for, not having seen him did not make her feel more relaxed. Instead, it gave her the sensation of living in close quarters with a tiger, knowing it was out there in the undergrowth somewhere, but never knowing when it would show itself. Though she had scolded herself soundly for her fanciful notions, the disquieting sensation lingered.

From what she had gathered from Rachel, his lordship was spending most of his time out of doors, supervising the work. Bea admitted herself surprised by this, having assumed he'd give orders to a steward and then leave them to it. The idea he might get his hands dirty had never occurred to her, though supervising was akin to bossing people about and perhaps that kind of thing gave him satisfaction, she thought, reminding herself he was untrustworthy, despicable and best avoided. Even so, curiosity nagged at her. She wondered what progress he had made and, worse, she wondered if he had seen her lovely parlour and what he thought of it. Did he admire the changes she had made, or did he dislike her taste and resent her making such changes to the home he'd known all his life?

She was still musing on this as Rachel departed, saying she must ensure their new cook had settled in. Bea let her go, not having any qualms about that. The woman, a sturdy no-nonsense female by the name of Mrs Kershaw, had excellent references for her previous twenty years, but had been forthcoming in explaining she had left her last employ where she had stayed for little more than a year, because the mistress was 'a featherbrained ninny who couldn't have organised her own toilette let alone a household.' Bea had taken to her at once and told the woman she thought they would get on marvellously, for she herself was a managing female who liked things all her own way. This had made Mrs Kershaw laugh roundly and agree they would enjoy some wonderful battles in the future. So, with mutual respect and understanding, Mrs Kershaw had begun giving orders and arranging the kitchen as she preferred it. Bea had left her to it, safe in the knowledge that they would eat well that night and poor Rachel need not run herself ragged any longer.

With one last look of pride at her new parlour, Bea went out, intending to go up and see if her new bedroom was finally finished as she was tired of the pokey little chamber she was using for the time being. She had just closed the door and taken two steps when the front door banged shut, a gust of chill air sweeping in as Rutherford appeared. Bea froze, suddenly struck with the urgent desire to escape back into her parlour. Telling herself not to be such a ninny, she stayed where she was. She was not about to hide from the blasted man, Bea watched as he handed his hat and coat to a footman. The butler, a tall and impressive looking fellow with iron grey hair and an air of consequence far greater than Rutherford's, informed him his valet was preparing a bath for him and his correspondence had been taken up to his rooms as the study had been packed up as he'd requested, ready for decorating.

Rutherford nodded his understanding and walked towards the stairs, halting as he noticed her watching him.

"My lady," he said, inclining his head.

"My lord," she replied, equally formal. "You've been outside," she said, rolling her eyes inwardly at the inane statement. That much had been obvious. Still, he did not smirk or make some irritating comment, merely nodded.

"There's much work to be done, but things are happening at last, which is heartening. I have an army of gardeners clearing undergrowth, and the stables, which have been in a sorry state indeed, are finally getting a new roof. I have missed having more horses about the place," he told her with a smile. "When I was a boy, the stables at Chalfont were some of the finest in the county. I'd like to think they could be again."

"A fine ambition," she remarked, thinking at least it was better than putting another notch on his bedpost or gambling the money away on the turn of a card.

"You like to ride, my lady?"

She nodded. "I do, very much."

"Then we must see about getting you a horse," he said, smiling at her again. "Do you ride well? If you will forgive such a question."

"I believe so. Certainly, my father always thought so, but perhaps he was biased. I miss riding with him very much. It always vexed me when I rode with my cousin, for she was too nervous to gallop or indulge in anything more than a trot. I have so missed the feeling of the wind rushing past and the sensation of flying across the countryside."

He stared at her with interest and looked as though he might say something else, but he seemed to think better of it. She thought he was about to turn away, heading up the stairs, when words she had not meant to speak flew from her mouth.

"We have a new cook, a Mrs Kershaw. She began this morning, turning the kitchens upside down. And the new staff, too," Bea remarked with a nervous laugh. "I believe we may have a fine dinner awaiting us tonight."

"Us?" he repeated, taking altogether the wrong part of her explanation and focusing on it.

"Well," Bea said, suddenly flustered. "Assuming you *are* eating? I never said we must eat together."

He studied her for a long moment, during which she felt oddly energised by his scrutiny.

"No, of course not." Rutherford returned a mocking smile and began to move away.

"Oh, very well!" Bea said impatiently, which had him turning around, his expression one of confusion. "I know! I know I said I would dine with you. There's no need to act as if I'm being unreasonable. Dinner is at six. Do not be late," she added tartly, before turning on her heel and going back into the parlour, despite having had no intention of doing so.

She leaned back against the door, closing her eyes and cursing herself.

"Beatrice Alice Huntingdon, you are a fool," she told herself in frustration, remembering belatedly that she was now Langley, not Huntingdon, which did nothing to soothe her temper.

Rutherford's expression of mingled amusement and bewilderment was still vivid in her mind, making her cheeks burn with mortification. Had he even realised they'd not shared a meal? Had he forgotten their arrangement so quickly? Did he no longer wish to torment her by enforcing the stupid rule? Did he not care to spend time with her? She did not know and ought not to care, either. She *ought* to be jumping with joy at an entire week passing without having to endure his company. What on earth had she been thinking?

Still, there was nothing to be done about it now. He had demanded they dine together three times a week, had he not, and she had agreed. If he did not wish to rouse himself in time to break his fast with her, so much the better, but she would not have him accusing her of reneging on their deal. That was all. That was the only reason she had forced the issue, for she certainly had no desire to spend a couple of awkward hours in his presence.

The realisation that she had several new gowns in bright colours to choose from, now she was finally out of mourning, mollified her somewhat. At least she need not face him looking a dowd.

❄ ❄ ❄ ❄ ❄

Justin stared at the parlour door as Bea closed it a little too forcefully. He frowned, somewhat taken aback by her outburst, but finding a pleased smile twitching at his lips. He did not doubt the only reason she had pressed the matter was because she feared him accusing her of reneging on their agreement and demanding some other, no doubt improper, recompense for the omission. Still, that she had requested he dine with her, when he had said and done nothing at all, was a victory so far as he was concerned. Whistling, he made his way up the stairs, feeling rather pleased with himself.

John was waiting for him as the butler had told him, having finally been returned to his station as valet, instead of chief cook and bottle washer. That the return of status pleased the man was obvious, as John was in an excellent humour and had enjoyed himself enormously by taking charge of reorganising and decorating Justin's rooms. Justin had privately hoped his wife might decide upon the decorating and furnishing of his chamber, but it had been a forlorn hope and one he'd not been stupid enough to press. He knew well enough what she must imagine had taken place in this space, assuming she had any idea *what* to imagine, but that she believed it depraved he did not doubt for a moment. His valet, too, was turned out as fine as fivepence in an expensive new suit of clothes that Justin had no qualms about paying for. Loyalty was rare in his experience, and he was not about to risk losing it by being tightfisted.

"There's hot water ready. If you'd like to sit down, my lord, I'll give you a shave. There's to be a fine dinner tonight, what with the new cook arriving, so you'd best dress appropriately and not show me up. We don't want Lady Rutherford to think you're completely lacking in manners, or that I can't turn you out proper, like."

Justin gave his valet a wry look. "John, either stop *my lording* me and speak your mind, or give the title the respect it deserves, even if I do not. The combination of my title and your plain speaking makes me feel like I'm being scolded by an overbearing nanny."

"Beggin' your pardon, my lord, but mayhap if you'd been scolded a bit more by an overbearing nanny, we wouldn't have gotten into this mess, now would we?"

"Is that the royal *we*, John?" Justin replied, stripping off his neckcloth, amused despite himself. "And I was scolded very soundly, I promise you. Nanny Gordon was the stuff of nightmares. I swear she would have frightened Wellington. She certainly skinned my arse frequently. I remember many times when I could not sit down for days on end. Spare the rod, spoil the child, John, you see. Look what good it did, what a fine specimen of manhood it produced," he said, gesturing to himself with a mocking smile.

John snorted as Justin sat back in the chair and tilted his head back. "Will you not tan your own brats' arses, then?"

Justin experienced an odd jolt of surprise at the question. He had told Bea that she might one day come to him, wanting him to give her a child, supposing she hadn't taken a lover to provide one for her by then. That idea made him feel hot and so nauseated he swallowed hard. Pushing the unsettling thought away, he considered the idea of his own children for the first time in his life. He'd assumed the line, and the title, would die with him—most likely in a gutter outside some gaming hell or brothel. But what if it didn't? What if Beatrice gave him an heir, what if she gave him a daughter too? His heart gave an erratic thud behind his ribs, and he wondered if he had abused his body so much with alcohol and burning the candle at both ends that he'd drop down dead from a heart attack one day soon. Justin realised then that he wanted to live to see his children, should his wife be foolish enough to give him any. He considered John's question and shook his head.

"No."

"Really?" John paused in the act of frothing up the shaving soap, looking at him in surprise. "You'd get the nanny to do it, then?" he asked, a note of disapproval in his voice.

Justin shook his head. "If anyone ever lays a hand on a child of mine, I shall dismiss them on the spot," he said crisply.

John stared at him for a long moment and then grinned. "Right you are, my lord."

❄ ❄ ❄ ❄ ❄

"Stop that!" Rachel scolded, swatting Bea's hand away from her newly arranged hair. "You'll spoil it and do stop fidgeting. Anyone would think you were going to dinner with his majesty, the state you're in."

"I am *not* in a state," Bea retorted indignantly, though she knew that was a lie.

No matter how many times she cursed herself for being an idiot, she still could not believe she had voluntarily arranged to have dinner with her husband. Her frustration with herself seemed to manifest itself in a desire to appear at her very best. She would not be put at a disadvantage by appearing anything but magnificent. If she believed doing her hair, donning jewellery and a beautiful gown were akin to dressing in a suit of armour—and she did—then she would appear ready for battle, and for anything the wretched man could throw at her.

Rachel made a scathing sound that suggested she remained unconvinced, but Bea ignored her, instead she turned this way and that before the looking glass, grateful the large cheval mirror had arrived earlier that day.

"Yes, you look every inch the countess, my Lady Rutherford," Rachel said, folding her arms and standing back to admire her handiwork. Bea regarded her maid in the mirror, noting the amused glint in her eyes. She turned to face her.

"You think I'm being ridiculous?"

Rachel studied her thoughtfully. "Not ridiculous," she said after a drawn-out pause.

"Well, you think something," Bea pressed, never having known Rachel not to say what she thought.

She waited while Rachel considered.

"I think you look very beautiful, and you should have a care what you wish for."

"What does that mean?" Bea asked, crinkling her nose in confusion.

"It means, if you are thinking to go downstairs and capture that man's attention, you'll likely do just that, so beware the consequences, that's what it means," Rachel said, wagging a finger at Bea.

"I do *not* want to capture his attention," Bea returned, feeling a flush of heat travel from her toes to her hair. "I simply will not have him treat me like some silly child. If he thinks to trick me again, or to tease me or… or play whatever games he has in mind, he will find I am not so foolish as to take part."

Rachel nodded, apparently agreeing with this, though Bea was uncertain of the look in her eyes. "Well, as long as you know what you're doing," she said mildly.

Bea was not the least bit certain, but she was not about to admit that to Rachel, or to anyone. She avoided answering by taking one last look in the mirror. "Thank you, Rachel. My hair looks lovely," she said with a smile, and escaped the bedroom before her maid could make any other unsettling observations.

She made her way down the stairs where the new butler, Morley, nodded a greeting. "Good evening, my lady."

"Good evening, Morley, is Lord Rutherford down yet?"

"No, my lady."

Bea nodded, relieved to have a few moments to settle her nerves. "I shall take a glass of Madeira in my parlour. Please show his lordship in when he comes down."

Morley nodded his understanding, and Bea left him to await her drink. The parlour looked splendid with the curtains drawn and the lamps lit, the firelight flickering in the hearth. She gave a little sigh of pleasure and took a moment to walk about the room, tweaking a cushion and straightening an ornament as she went. Settling down in one of a pair of comfortable chairs, covered in a lovely embroidered green and blue fabric, Bea sat by the fire. She faced the windows with the door to her back, imagining sitting there during the day, knowing she would be able to see the rolling hills outside. Bea smiled and allowed herself a moment of pure happiness at having such a beautiful room to relax in. A moment later, a footman appeared, bearing a bottle of Madeira and two glasses. He served her and left the bottle and the extra glass on a side table at her request.

Bea sipped her drink and was trying to remember the last time she had felt quite so content when the door opened, and her heart seemed to give a series of flurried beats in her chest. He was here. She knew it was Rutherford before he appeared in her line of vision, though she did not know how.

When he appeared before her, he stood for a moment, gazing around the room, taking it all in. Though she tried her best to appear nonchalant, Bea had to admit she was desperate for his opinion. It was the first room she had ever designed entirely by herself, with her own choices of colour and furniture and soft furnishings and, whilst she loved it, she was still a little uncertain what anyone else might think. Her husband, devil though he was, had been known in town not only for his excesses, but for having exquisite taste and an eye for fashion. If anyone should know anything about style, she supposed he ought.

"Well," he said, after an interminable interval that she was certain he strung out on purpose. "I can hardly believe it is the same room. You have a flair for colour and an eye for style, Beatrice. Congratulations. It's the kind of room one dreams of returning to when out in the cold and wet."

"Yes! Exactly that," Bea said eagerly, sitting forward in her seat despite having been determined not to let him charm her. All it had taken was a few words of flattery and she had caved in at once, drat him. Yet, his description was exactly what she had been aiming for. "I wanted a place where one could be warm and cosy and quite at ease when the rest of the world was unfriendly and cold."

He gave a soft laugh, slanting her a rueful smile. "I may never leave, in that case."

"You really like it, you're not just pouring the butter boat over me in the hopes of gaining something?" she demanded, frowning.

"My, my, you really do despise me," he remarked, reaching for the bottle and pouring himself a glass of Madeira.

Bea bit her lip, wishing she'd not been quite so forthright. "I beg your pardon, that was uncalled for, and no, I do not despise you. Not in the least. I simply do not know you and I trust you not at all."

"Ah, well, that's much better," he replied, grinning over the rim of his glass. *"À votre santé,"* he added, raising the glass to her before he drank.

Bea returned the salutation and sipped her own drink, watching through narrowed eyes as he made quick work of his glass and refilled it. He sat down opposite her, his long legs stretched out before him, crossed at the ankles. He wore dark trousers that fitted snugly about his thighs, highlighting a physique she found surprising considering his indolent lifestyle. The waistcoat and coat were likewise dark, a deep navy blue, she thought, though it was hard to tell between blue and black in the lamplight. Either way, the severe colour highlighted his fair hair and sharp bone structure, a foil for his golden good looks. He appeared to her eye in the light of a dissipated angel, Lucifer in the weeks just after the fall. A lazy smile curved his sinful mouth and Bea realised she'd been staring. Flushing hotly, she looked away.

A knock at the door saved her from any off colour remark he would surely have made about her perusal of his person, and Morley announced dinner.

Bea set down her glass and got up, a little surprised and unnerved, when she found Rutherford at her elbow, ready to escort her in. It was on the tip of her tongue to refuse him, but it seemed churlish, for he was being courteous, the least she could do was meet him halfway. So she placed her hand on his sleeve, immediately aware of the strength in the arm beneath her fingers.

"How is your shoulder?" she asked him, looking up at him.

If he resented the reminder of his ignominious duel and subsequent exile from town, he did not show it. "It mends," he said, leading her out of the parlour. "It still aches rather, but the sawbones did a decent job patching me up and had a fair hand with a needle, for it seems to be a neat job. John is a conscientious nursemaid who frets over the wound too, so there is no chance of it getting inflamed again."

"I'm glad," she replied politely.

He snorted at that. "No, you're not. It would have been perfect for you if I'd married you, got an infection in my blood and turned up my toes. A wife and a widow within a week. How merry you would have been."

"That is an appalling thing to say!" Bea said in outrage, glaring at him and trying to forget she had once thought exactly that.

"It is. True, though," he replied, a wicked glint sparkling in his eyes.

Despite her intention not to let him charm her, the dreadful comment tickled her, and she could not quite smother the choked laughter that caught her off guard.

"It is," she admitted, and then covered her mouth with her hand, not quite believing she had said such an awful thing.

Rutherford laughed, shaking his head. "Well, I hope I have not been such an appalling husband after our first days of marriage that you still wish me six feet under."

His words were still teasing but Bea wondered if there was a real question there.

"Of course not," she said, shaking her head. "Indeed, funning aside, I never wished such a fate upon you. Only that you leave me in peace. Your lifestyle is not one I admire, and I wish no part in it."

They had reached the dining room by then and he did not answer as footmen hurried to pull out their chairs. To Bea's mingled relief and dismay, she realised she was sitting by his side at the head of the table. Whilst shouting up and down the enormous length of the dining room would have been ridiculous, this seemed rather too intimate, and once again she wished she had kept her blasted mouth shut.

They sat and the conversation that followed was stilted until the white soup was removed and a haricot of lamb, fish with white wine and mushrooms, a vegetable pie and assorted pickles were served. Then Rutherford dismissed the footmen, leaving them to dine in private.

"You dislike having servants around?" Bea asked, somewhat surprised. Most of the nobility she had experience of treated servants like they were merely part of the furniture, paying them no more mind than they might a side table. Her father had not been one of them and they had never eaten so formally at home. Her uncle had been another matter.

"Servants gossip, even the best of them," Rutherford said, making a pleased sound as he sampled the lamb. "This is excellent."

Bea smiled and nodded. "I knew Mrs Kershaw would be splendid. She brought fresh baked rolls and a pot of her own jam to the interview," she said with a laugh.

"They were good?"

"The rolls were like little puffs of air, so light it was a wonder they did not float off, and the jam was heavenly."

"What kind of jam?"

"Bramble," Bea replied, almost sighing with pleasure as she tasted the fish in white wine sauce. It was light and perfectly seasoned, the mushrooms giving an exquisite earthy note to the dish.

"Is there any left?" Rutherford asked, pausing with a forkful of lamb suspended in midair.

"I-I don't know," Bea asked in surprise. "I can ask. Why?"

"It's my favourite thing in the world," he admitted ruefully. "Good bread, thick butter and bramble jam. If ever I was given cause to request my last ever meal on earth, that would be it."

"Bread and jam?" she said, somewhat sceptically.

He nodded, laughing at her expression. "My tastes are not so peculiar and wild as you might imagine. Indeed, I find I am happier this evening than I can remember being for many years, so I thank you for that."

Bea almost choked on the mouthful of food she'd just taken. As it was, she swallowed with difficulty, staring at him, her heart hammering. "Don't do that."

Rutherford looked up from his plate, frowning. "Do what?" he asked in confusion.

Bea pushed back her chair, getting to her feet. "I agreed to dine with you, to be civil with you, but on the condition we were polite. You wanted friendship, and I said no, that was a bad idea, but *this*… this intimacy you try to foist upon me, the idea that I have made you happy with a bit of inane conversation when you are used to heaven alone knows what exotic pleasures—" She sucked in a breath, trying to still her heart which was beating too hard, too fast. "I beg you will not treat me with such contempt. I am not a fool."

With that, she turned and strode towards the door. Rutherford got to his feet, his chair screeching on the polished parquet as he followed, grabbing her arm.

"Not so fast, lady wife," he said, and she heard a thread of anger in his voice, a steely note that made her skin prickle with alarm. "Why are you so damned determined to see me as a monster? Must you believe every word ever written about me? Is there no room for doubt in that well-protected heart of yours? I spoke true, blast you. I *am* happy, and yes, it was a little inane conversation, on an evening spent in my own home, with good food and my beautiful wife beside me, that did it. If you believe me too shallow, too loathsome and sunk in depravity to find pleasure in such things, then so be it, but it's true all the same and I shall not take it back!"

With that, he released his grip on her arm and returned to the table. He sat down, snatching up his wineglass and taking a large swallow.

Bea stood frozen to the spot, uncertain of what to do, what to think. He sounded entirely sincere, but could this also be part of a long-term plan to wriggle his way into her affections? But why would he bother? Was he so desperate to make a conquest of her, just to prove a point? Could a man the *ton* had labelled a rake and a rogue for so many years, really be worthy of a second chance?

Cautiously, she returned to her seat. Her hands shook a little as she reached for her wine and took a sip.

"I beg your pardon," he said stiffly and, when she looked at him, she found him staring straight ahead. "I ought not to have spoken so to you. I can hardly blame you for your contempt. I earned every bit of it with years of dedicated work."

The words were harsh and bitter, filled with self-loathing.

Bea cast around for something to say but found nothing. Her instincts told her he was genuinely upset, but the past months of finding herself alone and powerless at the hands of her uncle had made her overly cautious, and perhaps a little callous.

"I will leave you to eat your dinner in peace," he said suddenly, pushing back his chair.

Before she had made a conscious decision to do so, Bea's hand shot out and she grasped his arm. "Wait."

Rutherford stilled, his blue eyes fixed on her, a look there she could not read and did not wish to interpret.

"Don't go," she said, releasing his arm, as the feel of it beneath her hand was giving her the oddest sensation.

"There is no need to suffer my company for the sake of good manners," he said, his voice almost a growl.

"I am doing no such thing. I—" Bea took a breath and said the words in a rush, before she could think better of it. "I apologise."

His expression was one of such incredulity that Bea could not help but smile.

"I *am* capable of apologising when I'm wrong."

He gave a little huff of laughter. "What if you're not wrong? What if this is all part of an elaborate plan to get into your good graces?"

"Is it?" she asked him, watching his face carefully.

He pondered the question, turning his wineglass back and forth. "Yes and no," he said at length.

Bea frowned. "Is that a confession?"

He smiled at her. "There's no dastardly plot, Beatrice. I have no desire to hurt or manipulate you, but I would like to be in your good graces. I would very much like it if my wife thought of me with something less than revulsion. I want to be considered at the very least as a friend, but… perhaps even someone to rely upon."

Bea stared at him, wanting to believe him. He sounded so sincere, and she knew her stupid heart was eager to give him the chance he desired, but she had no wish to be hurt any further than she had been. Her father's death had shattered her, then her uncle's bullying and machinations had undermined the idea that there was anyone left in the world in whom she could put her trust. Even Rachel, of whom she was so fond, was paid to stay by her side, though she had remained when she might have found an easier position, Bea reminded herself. But Rutherford's character was said by all to be so thoroughly black, surely she would be a fool indeed to put her trust in such an unworthy man.

"What you ask is no small thing, my lord," she said, forcing herself to look at him as she spoke.

His blue eyes glittered, his gaze intent and his attention absolutely focused upon her, which was at once nerve-wracking and somehow thrilling. That this man who had cut a swathe through the women of the *ton*, none of whom had captured his interest for more than a fleeting moment, might truly desire her good opinion, her regard, might want *her* attention focused upon him, well that was a heady temptation and one she could not allow herself to be seduced by.

"I have no reason in the world to trust you, every reason to believe you will disappoint me. I have no one left in the world to whom I might turn. My only living family has betrayed me so vilely I never wish to see them again. I am alone, and the temptation to put my trust in you is one I dare not give in to. I do not wish for you to hurt me."

The light that had shone in his eyes dimmed at her words. "I understand," he said, nodding. "I know I ask too much. I have always asked too much, but perhaps, in time, I might prove to you I am not so black as I have been painted. Perhaps in time, you might give me that chance?"

Bea considered this. "If you wish to be my friend, then treat me as such. Do not try to woo me. Speak to me as… as you might speak to John."

His eyebrows rose at that, and she hurried on.

"Well, not John, perhaps. A sister," she suggested, pleased with the idea. "Treat me as a sister and perhaps, in time, I shall feel content to be your friend."

"A sister," he replied sceptically. "I never had a sister. I would not know how to begin."

"An aunt, then."

He gave a choked laugh. "Good God, my Aunt Sophronia seemed like Methuselah to me even when I was a lad. She's been dead for two decades. I promise you, you do not have the slightest thing in common."

She smiled, shaking her head. "I believe you take my meaning, however."

He nodded. "I do, and I promise to try, though if you wish such treatment, I beg you will not come down to dinner dressed so splendidly, for you will test the limits of my willpower most dreadfully."

"You are doing it now!" she protested, throwing up her hands.

"So I am," he remarked in dismay. "Very well. We will start over. Beatrice, would you pass me that pie? It looks delicious and I am famished."

Beatrice slid the plate over to him, watching as he helped himself to a large slice. He took a mouthful and nodded his approval.

"Oh, that's good. You must have some and tell me what rooms you are planning on attacking next. What do you have in mind?"

For a moment, Bea hesitated as he served her a slice of pie, watching him cautiously, but if he was prepared to do as she had asked, then she could at least have a civilised conversation with him.

"Well?" he pressed. "Tell me everything you have planned."

And so she did.

Chapter 7

8th November 1820.

Rutherford kept his word. He rose early and took breakfast with her, and they would share their plans for the day. Then Bea rarely saw him again, though sometimes she would glance out of a window and spy him out in the gardens. He would grin and raise a hand to wave at her and Bea would wave back. Other than that, they only spoke at dinner. They had shared three more dinners, and Bea was pleasantly surprised by how well each had gone. They discussed the progress they had made, and the merits or failings of the staff with whom they were working. But they also discussed books, the theatre, music, and a wide range of topics, including politics.

He even discussed the Radical War and the recent execution of two of the men involved in the uprising at Bonnybridge. Bea had never had a man other than her father give her a proper conversation about such topics, for such things could not be discussed with women, certainly not unmarried women, in polite society. Her uncle would never have allowed her to have an opinion about such things. Yet Rutherford treated her as an equal, as though she had a brain in her head. He listened to her point of view and did not immediately squash her ideas, but considered them, and that was a rather thrilling experience.

As their peaceful coexistence continued, the house took shape, one room at a time. Rutherford seemed even more eager than she to get the work done and he hired more staff, an army of maids and workmen thronging the old place so that it felt as if it were a giant anthill, seething with activity. Walking from one room to another was perilous, for you might turn a corner and run straight into a maid with a mop and bucket, or a painter, or men hefting the newly acquired bits of furniture into place. It was exciting and exhausting and sometimes it seemed as if there was not a quiet corner to be found anywhere.

Such a hive of activity was bound to stir interest in the local area, however, the news that the wickedest rake in England had not only married, but married money, became a predictable subject of conversation. All the local shopkeepers were eager for the earl to patronise their premises, and anyone looking for work would appear on the doorstep of Chalfont. So, it was inevitable that her uncle would eventually put two and two together.

Though the butler had been instructed from the outset that her uncle, Lord Worth, was under no circumstances to be allowed into the house, it did not stop the viscount from standing on the doorstep and demanding to see Bea. His voice was loud and angry enough to reach her parlour with ease.

"Just let him bellow, my lady," Rachel advised, giving Bea's hand a squeeze as she came out and dithered in the hallway. "He'll get bored and go away soon enough."

Bea knew that was true, but the idea her uncle might believe her too afraid to face him rankled. "No. He'll only come back again. Better I get it over with," Bea said, though her heart was beating too hard, too fast.

Steeling her nerve, she put up her chin, reminding herself that she was the Countess of Rutherford, and her uncle had no hold over her. Not any longer.

Bea gestured to Morley, who opened the door, and she strode out to stand on the top step. From here, she could look down upon her uncle, and that was not an unpleasant sensation.

"You are not welcome here," she told him, relieved that her voice barely trembled.

Her uncle, who had paused his shouting, turned at the sound of her voice. "You little bitch!" he said furiously, stalking up the stairs towards her. "I suppose you think you're very clever, you scheming little whore."

Bea jolted, never having been spoken to so in all her life. "If you cannot keep a civil tongue in your head, we have nothing left to say to each other," she said, about to turn but her uncle grasped hold of her wrist, his grip bruising.

"Not so fast. You owe me, Beatrice. That money ought to have been mine, if your father had not been such a besotted fool over you. I demand you give me what is mine."

Bea stared at him, so incredulous that for a moment she forgot to be afraid. "That money now belongs to my husband," she said with icy disdain, and not entirely truthfully, but she was not about to tell him of their deal.

"That disgusting excuse for a man," Charles said in contempt, sneering at her. "You'll be a laughingstock for having married such a vile libertine, I hope you realise."

Bea stared at her uncle, never having experienced a surge of hatred so overwhelming as she did in that moment. "That vile libertine has treated me with respect. He took me in and has dealt with me fairly and with more kindness than I believed possible, yet my family, my *dear* uncle, purposely arranged a situation where a loathsome toad of a man could force his attentions on me until he bullied me into agreeing to wed him. Which of those men do you think worthy of my regard, and which of my unending scorn and disgust?" she demanded, the contempt in her voice so audible her uncle flushed.

His grip on her wrist tightened though, twisting, and Bea gave a cry of pain.

"I'll have that money, Beatrice," he growled. "You owe——"

"Take your damned hands off my wife!"

The words thundered in her ears, roared with such fury even Bea jumped. Her uncle turned but did not release his hold on her.

"Rutherford!" Bea exclaimed, relief flooding her at the sight of her husband running up the steps towards them.

"I said release her!" he bellowed, and Bea gasped at the rage flashing in his eyes.

Her uncle was a large man but run to fat and, being far older than Rutherford, in the prime of life no longer. He let go of Bea and glared at the earl who stalked up to him and pushed him hard, making Uncle Charles stagger backwards.

"If you were not so decrepit, I should knock you down this second, but if you ever, *ever* lay a finger on her again, I *shall* kill you," Rutherford said, his voice so cold and so certain Bea shivered.

"Shall you indeed?" Charles replied, with more bravado than Bea expected, for it was clear Rutherford could flatten him if he chose to do so. "You did not come off so well in your last meeting, I understand," he said with a sneer.

"I deloped," Rutherford said, his voice low. "You may be sure I shall not do so for you."

"I shall contact my lawyers," her uncle snarled, glaring between them. "I shall get the marriage annulled."

"On what grounds?" Rutherford demanded incredulously. "Beatrice is of age, she needed no permission from you, and if you think the marriage has not been thoroughly consummated, you are a bigger fool than I reckoned upon. You'll be laughed out of court if you try that one," he added with a smirk. "After all, my reputation precedes me."

"You won't get away with this, Beatrice," Uncle Charles growled, his face flushed with anger. He didn't look well, his eyes too bright, almost febrile. "I'll have that money yet!"

Rutherford had clearly had enough. Taking hold of Charles' arm, he wrenched it up behind his back and forced him down the steps.

"Unhand me, you bastard!" Charles raged, struggling to no effect as Rutherford proved just how outmatched he was.

Rutherford marched the man down the steps, practically throwing him headfirst into his carriage. "Get him out of here," he bellowed to the footmen who had been watching with wide eyes, wondering whether to interfere. "And make sure he's never allowed to set foot on the estate again. Anyone who permits it will face instant dismissal. Is that understood?"

The men nodded and hurried to manhandle her uncle into the carriage, closing the door on him.

Bea watched from the top of the steps with a sense of unreality until the carriage moved away, back down the path.

Rutherford turned and hurried up to her. "Beatrice? Are you well? Did he hurt you?"

Bea shook her head.

"Lord, you're shaking," he said in dismay, shrugging out of his coat. He put it around her shoulders and guided her inside. "Come on, sweetheart. You're tougher than that vile bully can ever understand. Don't let him upset you. You won, remember? You outsmarted him and got everything you wanted—well, not everything, you got *me*, but all the same, you thwarted his disgusting plans."

He guided her inside and back to her lovely parlour where the fire was blazing.

"Come, sit down. I'll fetch you a glass of brandy," he said, manoeuvring her to her favourite chair.

"I'm q-quite all right," she protested, sitting down with a thud.

"Of course you are," Rutherford said. "I never thought anything different. Still, such an ugly scene is upsetting for anyone. It upset *me*."

Bea looked up at him. "Thank you," she said, letting out a shaky breath. "I swear I was never so pleased to see anyone in my whole life."

He returned a crooked smile. "Ah, well. At least I'm good for something, eh?"

Bea opened her mouth to protest the comment, but he turned away to pour her a glass of brandy, and she realised she did not know what it was she wished to say, so she said nothing.

Rutherford returned with the glass and then frowned as he realised she was cradling her wrist. He set the brandy down on a side table and knelt beside her.

"Show me," he said, gesturing to it.

Bea lifted her arm and uncovered her wrist. He gently tugged up her sleeve to reveal that it was red and angry, bruises already appearing on her fair skin. Rutherford's face darkened, a look in his eyes that frightened her a little.

"I ought to have killed him then and there," he growled. "He'll pay for that, Beatrice, I swear it. I—"

"No!" she exclaimed, shaking her head. "No, please. I want no more upset, no fighting, no duel. Please, Rutherford, promise me."

A muscle ticked in his jaw, but he met her eyes and gave a taut nod. "Very well, but if he ever lays a finger on you again, if he comes within a mile of you, I shan't keep that promise."

Bea smiled, touched and reassured by his vehemence. Whilst she had not believed he would stand back and allow her uncle to abuse her, she had not expected to be protected so fiercely.

"Thank you, Rutherford, for what you did for me," she said, staring at him. "I knew everything would be all right the moment you appeared, and it was. I'm so glad you were there."

To her surprise, a tinge of colour crested his high cheekbones. "So am I," he said softly. "Shall I call Rachel for you? You'd best see to your wrist."

Bea nodded, and he smiled. For a moment she saw the man he might have been if he'd not thrown everything away for a life of gambling and scandal, if he'd not chosen pleasure over a desire to make something of himself, his life. But perhaps he simply didn't know better. His mother had died when he was a baby, and from the little she had heard of his father, he was no fit person to be a role model for an impressionable boy. Perhaps Rutherford really was a good man, deep inside. Perhaps he'd only needed a reason to change his behaviour, and he'd not had that before. Though she knew, *knew*, she would regret her action, she could not deny the impulse to lean forward and press a kiss to his cheek. "Thank you, my knight in shining armour."

He stilled, gazing at her in obvious shock. "The armour is tarnished. Beyond repair, remember," he replied, something that sounded like regret in his voice.

"Tarnished, certainly," Bea agreed. "But perhaps it might be mended, given time and a lot of elbow grease."

He laughed at that, the endearing crooked smile she was becoming familiar with making an appearance. "How much elbow grease?" he demanded suspiciously.

"A *lot*," she repeated, her voice firm.

He snorted, shaking his head, and then got to his feet. "Drink your brandy, little Boudicca, I shall fetch Rachel to tend your battle scars."

With that, he went out of the room, leaving Bea feeling oddly happy despite the stresses of the day.

❄ ❄ ❄ ❄ ❄

Justin dithered in Bea's parlour later that same day, awaiting her appearance for one of their thrice weekly dinners. He'd felt strangely restless and out of sorts since the scene with her uncle. No. That wasn't true. He'd wanted to kill Viscount Worth and would have happily gone after him with that intention in mind upon seeing her lovely skin so abraded and bruised. Even now, rage burned in his guts at the damage her uncle had done, but that wasn't what had him in a stew. For her sake, he could put that aside… assuming the bastard never bothered them again. No, the thing that had him all on edge and pacing the room with nervous impatience to see her again, had been the kiss.

He told himself he was being ridiculous. It had hardly been a kiss at all. No doubt she considered it a sisterly peck on the cheek. It *had* been a sisterly peck on the cheek! She had asked him to treat her like a sister, after all. Justin wondered if she had the slightest idea how hard it was to do as she asked, when every time he saw her, he became more and more obsessed with the idea of making her his own.

He'd tried to step back and consider his feelings impassively. It was logical to suppose that he would desire the woman he was sharing a house with. In the first place, she was a desirable woman. There was no question of that, though she was by no means the most beautiful female he'd ever seen. Some of the highflyers he'd spent time with had possessed the kind of beauty that poets wrote sonnets about, that might drive a man mad if he was fool enough to give his heart into their keeping. Justin had never been that man. His heart had never once been in danger. He'd been friends with many of his lovers, at least for the time the affair lasted. Somehow, he had never gained the knack of leaving gracefully. When they discovered they really could not hold him, that they were not the one who could keep his attention, they became resentful, despite having been told time and again what his rules were.

He'd had many parting gifts thrown at him, for he was always generous, even when his pockets were to let. Too generous, according to John, but the women had given something of themselves, and he had given so little of himself it seemed like he owed them that much. Oh, he'd given them his time, his attention, had done everything he could to ensure their pleasure, but he'd always kept himself aloof, almost a voyeur of his own life, remote, detached. He was not detached where Beatrice was concerned. The remoteness that had kept him going through the years seemed to have deserted him the moment she had appeared before him, walking into danger with her head high and her eyes flashing with scorn. Coolly making a bargain with the devil as if she did it every day, instead of in the hours after having fled her uncle's house and escaping the abuse she had been promised there.

God, but she was brave and strong, and yet so lovely and fragile he had the appalling urge to want to keep her safe from everything. Not just from her uncle either, but from anything, any person or event that might so much as ruffle her composure. He wanted to ensure her comfort and buy her gifts to make her smile. What *was* wrong with him? He was turning into a blasted mooncalf after two decades as a devoted rake.

He told himself he was simply out of sorts after a traumatic period in his life, combined with not having bedded a woman for far too long. The confrontation with Lavinia's husband had been worse than even he had imagined, and he'd known it would be bad. Lavinia might have told him it would not be so dreadful, but he was not a fool. He'd known better than she what he was doing. Not that he blamed her; she had been desperate and, in her desperation, she had played down her husband's wrath. Robert was a coward, she'd said, he would never challenge him to a duel. *Ha!* Not that it would have changed anything. Justin had known and had done what he always did—exactly what he wanted to do and damn the consequences. Well, the consequences had been terrible. Really, *really* terrible, and he'd almost died, and the entire world now believed him the worst kind of libertine. At least before they had accepted him because he was amusing and handsome and he knew how to dress and, even if he hadn't a feather to fly with, he was still an earl. That meant something. Or it had.

But he had broken the rules, those unspoken rules that all gentlemen knew existed, even if they never acknowledged them, and that had been his undoing. Nevermind that Lavinia's husband had been the real villain. Everyone knew it, but that was behind closed doors and was therefore not their affair. They hadn't wanted to look at reality, had not wanted to see. So, Justin had done the only thing he could do and forced the bastard's hand. In public. Where he could not escape the consequences. Sadly, Justin hadn't escaped them either. So much for doing the honourable thing.

'No good deed goes unpunished' was a phrase his father had been fond of and had repeated often in the weeks they had spent together. It wasn't until recently that Justin had truly appreciated what those words meant. Before Lavinia he had taken his pleasure where and when he liked, he had lived precariously, but well enough, depending on whether the cards or the horses favoured him, or if his ladylove of the moment was inclined to indulge him with expensive gifts. Lavinia's plight had prompted a fleeting moment of chivalry, a desire to do something honourable that he had been paying for ever since.

Now, he was exiled from the world he had dwelled in since he was old enough to take his place in it. He'd been banished from everything that was familiar, and his life-raft was his old home, finally being raised from the ashes of decay and neglect and rising like a phoenix, renewed and beautiful once more. Beatrice shared the wonder of that metamorphosis with him, so it stood to reason a bond would exist between them. Though it had been through no fault of her own, she too had been hurt and knocked about by the vicissitudes of life and so he found in her a reflection of his own pain. It was only to be expected that he was drawn to her, that he wanted to seek comfort in her company, in her arms… in her bed. Only to be expected, he repeated urgently, trying and failing to keep his mind from the inevitable path it would take. He swallowed, lurid pictures appearing in his mind's eye, of her delicate arms about his neck, of her unbound hair sliding over his naked skin, of— *No.*

No, he'd made a promise and, for once in his miserable life, he was going to keep it.

He looked up as the door opened and Beatrice came in, and it was as if the universe had stepped in and sent a message even he could not find ambiguous, for she was dressed in a gown of white satin. It was beautifully embroidered with tiny blue flowers and embellished with seed pearls and blonde lace and made her look so pure and virginal the back of his neck burned with shame for the thoughts he'd been having about her just seconds earlier. Yet his depraved mind only desired her more, wanted her with greater urgency. She was his wife, a voice in the back of his head reminded him. *His wife.*

"Good evening, my lord. I hope I am not late. Have I kept you waiting?" she asked, glancing at the mantel clock.

"Not in the least, and it is not exactly a hardship to wait for you in this lovely room. I hope you do not mind me making use of it. I do not wish to trespass upon your private space."

"Of course not." She waved this away, which he found heartening until she added, "I can hardly complain when I have not yet seen fit to decorate your own parlour, but you may be certain I shall begin it next week. Now that the study is complete, your parlour and the library will be my next project."

"Ah, then you will soon be rid of me," he said, his tone rather more brittle than he'd intended.

She paused, giving him an oddly penetrating look. "I meant no insult," she said cautiously.

Justin shook off his irritation and forced a smile. "Of course not. None taken," he said, setting down his empty glass. "Shall we go through?"

Beatrice nodded, accepting his proffered arm, and he escorted her out and through to the breakfast room. It was serving as their dining room too until that was habitable again.

"I prefer eating in here to that great draughty hall," Beatrice said as a footman held her chair for her. "It's far cosier."

"It is," Justin agreed, taking his own place beside her. "Which is just as well. I was informed earlier we have been lucky the chimney hasn't fallen on our heads while we were dining."

Beatrice pulled a face and nodded as she accepted a glass of wine. "I know. Did you see how much soot came down, not to mention half a ton of bricks? It was a wonder no one was hurt. The workmen were black from head to toe, the poor fellows. Will it be a dreadfully expensive repair?"

Justin shrugged. "Fairly dreadful, but better it was discovered, and the job done properly. As you say, no one was hurt, and the work was unavoidable as I wish the house to remain standing for generations to come."

She fell silent, a slight flush of rose colouring her porcelain skin that Justin wondered at until he recalled his words. *For generations to come.* Of course, there would be no generations to come if she did not accept him as her husband. He thought about apologising but decided against it. No doubt it would only make her increasingly ill at ease.

The soup course was served, giving them a moment to overcome the slightly tense atmosphere. Justin waved the servants away, telling them not to return until he summoned them, and watched his wife covertly, his gaze drawn to the elegant line of her lovely neck, to the simple string of pearls she had looped around her throat. He had never seen her wear elaborate jewellery, though he supposed she'd hardly had a moment to shop for such things. Everything she'd owned must have, by necessity, been left behind at her uncle's house when she had fled. He frowned at that, wondering what treasures she was missing, what mementoes of her beloved father she had been forced to abandon. The idea rankled. That bastard had taken enough from Beatrice, Justin would not allow him to keep that which did not belong to him.

"Would you be free tomorrow morning?" he asked her, so suddenly she started.

"Oh, I… Yes, perhaps. At least, I could be if it is something important. I had planned to discuss the work to be done in the library and write some letters. Do you know, I had a reply from a dear friend of mine this morning. I wrote a few days ago to explain a little of what had happened to me, and she wrote back at once. Isn't that wonderful? All this time, I believed I had been forgotten, but it was not true. At least… not entirely."

"Not entirely?" Justin queried, momentarily diverted by the glimmer of doubt he saw in her eyes, the anxious way her brows tugged together.

"I'm being silly," she said with a shake of her head that made her curls bounce.

"I doubt that. Go on, say what you are thinking. You cannot shock me, remember? I'm entirely wicked and quite unshockable."

She laughed a little at that, but her expression became serious once more. "Well, it's just that Julia was my best friend in the world. I believed we told each other everything, shared our hopes and dreams and… and I cannot help but think that if she was suddenly taken away to live with a relation after the death of her father, I would do more than write a few letters and then give up when I got no reply."

Justin smiled, though his heart ached for her, understanding at once what she meant. "Of course you would. You would have gone to see for yourself, no matter if she had been taken to live in the wilds of the Scottish Highlands. You would have gone and knocked down the door until someone presented your friend to you and you were assured of her wellbeing."

She flushed, staring at him, and he realised she believed he was mocking her.

"I mean what I say, Beatrice," he said in a hurry, setting down his spoon. "You are the kind of person other people rely on. You are good and true and honest, and if you give your word, you keep it. If I had ever lived the kind of life where I'd had proper friends, I should have wanted one like that, like you."

Beatrice held his gaze for a long moment and then her lovely mouth curved up. The smile did something odd to his heart, making it feel at once light and too full, as though it would escape the confines of his chest. "You do have one like that," she said softly.

He would have smiled if his throat hadn't ached so, if the words hadn't touched upon some raw, private space he had kept hidden from the world, even from himself. What was she doing to him? Little by little, she was unravelling everything that held him together. All the untidily stitched repairs to his soul, to his peace of mind, to the ragged empty spaces that would yawn open if he let them were coming undone. He forced down the panicky sensation in his gut and told himself he was becoming overwrought. She had offered him friendship, for heaven's sake, *friendship,* not a place in her bed. Why was he getting in such a lather over being friends with his own wife?

"What did you want of me?"

He jumped guiltily, gazing at her, wondering if she had read something in his face that had shown he wanted far more than mere friendship, but she only smiled.

"You asked if I was free in the morning," she reminded him.

Oh. Justin nodded, trying to pull himself together. "Yes, I… I did."

For the love of God, are you going to let her wreck you? demanded the voice in his head. He shook it off, remembering what it had been he'd wanted to do for her, for this woman who was foolish enough to be his friend when the world and his wife thought him sunk too low to ever show his face again.

"Why?" she prompted, giving him a look that suggested she thought he was acting rather oddly. He didn't blame her.

"Because I want to take you back to your uncle's house," he said, realising too late that had been a clumsy explanation.

Her spoon fell with a clatter, and she stared at him in shock.

"No! Not… *no*, I only meant to recover the things that you left behind," he said in a rush, reaching out and covering her hand with his. The action was instinctive, the urge to reassure her, to comfort her, but now his hand rested atop hers, feeling the cool, soft skin beneath his palm, and the way she trembled.

"The things I left behind?" she repeated, gazing at him in confusion.

"It's just I was thinking that you left with such haste, you must have left things behind. Clothes and jewellery? Perhaps things that you treasured and would want beside you now you are settled. Your uncle has no right to them, and you should have them back. If you wish for me to go alone and fetch them for you, you need only provide me with a list, and I shall see it done. But I thought… I thought perhaps you would wish…"

"Yes!"

Her eyes glittered with a vibrancy he'd never seen before, excitement and determination and… pride? He wasn't sure, but that she was pleased he did not doubt.

"You would really do that for me?" she asked, sounding strangely breathless.

He smiled at her, the desire to tell her he would do anything for her hard to hold back, but he was not ready to make such a damned fool of himself. Not when she would think he only wished to bed her. He *did* wish it, the voice in his head said emphatically, but he knew himself too well not to recognise an attempt at delusion.

"I would. I would be glad to," he told her, the only words he would allow himself to speak.

She turned her hand beneath his and squeezed his fingers. "Thank you, Rutherford. Thank you very much."

"Justin," he said, his voice sounding strange to his own ears. "Please, call me Justin."

"Thank you, Justin," she repeated, looking a little uncertain but saying it anyway.

Elation filled his chest, triumph at having won something of true value, giving him a sense of pride, a kind of happiness she had never experienced before.

"You're very welcome, Beatrice."

She slid her hand free and turned her attention back to her soup, but the sensation lingered throughout the meal, making him feel like a king.

Chapter 8

9th November 1820.

Beatrice took breakfast in her room the next morning, not yet ready to face Rutherford. No… *Justin*. He had asked her to call him Justin, and she had agreed. She still did not know if she was being an unutterable fool, but he had sought to do something for her, not only a kindness, but something more than that. He was returning her power to her, the power to act in her own best interests, which her uncle had sought to steal away. That he had thought of that and given her the choice of whether to send him in her stead or for her to go with him, well, it had shaken her. It had made her look at her husband and wonder if this was the man he really was. She wanted it to be. To her shame, she wanted it more every day.

Bea had known it was a terrible idea to spend time with him, to share breakfasts and dinners together, where they could discuss their day, their shared interests, their little triumphs and disasters. It engendered familiarity, intimacy, and a desire to further a friendship she knew was dangerous. The Earl of Rutherford might well be a good man, despite all the gossip to the contrary. He might not resemble the villain the ton had painted him as of late, but that did not mean he would be a good husband, it did not mean he would be faithful. Which meant if she allowed herself to care for him, enough to risk a marriage that was more than just a sharing of a name and a property, she would get her heart broken.

There was little point in denying it. Justin Langley, the Earl of Rutherford, was charming, handsome, compelling, witty, and thoughtful, and the more time she spent in his company, the more she craved it. *Fool. Stupid, stupid fool.*

Yet how could she have done otherwise? If he was being courteous, it ill-behoved her to throw that back in his face, to act cruelly and treat him with contempt, though it would have been the sensible thing to do.

"Oh, Bea, you are on the path to a broken heart," she told herself wretchedly.

Despite her anxiety, her mingled excitement and terror for the coming morning was undiminished, galvanising her into jumping out of bed the moment she had finished eating. She dressed with care, choosing one of the new gowns that had arrived the day before. It was a shagreen pink gros de Naples silk and quite *a la mode.*

"Your uncle will gnash his teeth considering the pretty penny that outfit will have cost," Rachel said impishly, giving her a conspiratorial smile.

Bea laughed, despite the quiver of anxiety in her belly. The porridge she had eaten was not sitting comfortably this morning. "I should hope so too," she remarked, with more insouciance than she was feeling.

"John is going with you, and a dozen footmen too, so there's no need to be anxious. There will be no question of the horrid man touching you," Rachel said. "John knows better than to let any harm befall you, for he'll have me to answer to."

Bea regarded her maid with interest. She had known Justin would ensure her safety, for he had told her so before she had retired for the night. No, the interesting part had been the way Rachel had said *John.* Not *that fellow,* or *Rutherford's valet.*

"You trust him to look after me, then?" she asked casually, watching Rachel's face.

Rachel smiled and nodded. "I reckon so. He's strong, for one thing, and for reasons I don't understand, he thinks the world of his lordship. He says you've changed Rutherford for the better and so he's all for it. Reckons you'll be the making of him and so he thinks highly of you, too."

"He really said I've changed Rutherford?" Bea said in surprise, never having believed the surly valet would have approved of her.

"He did, and he's been with Rutherford since he were not much more than a lad. Been together through thick and thin, by all accounts."

"They have?" Bea asked, interested in the conversation for an entirely different reason now.

Rachel nodded, moving forward with a frown to tweak Bea's coiffure. "John said he'd not been paid for nearly a year before you arrived, but he stayed with his lordship all the same. He says Rutherford got a rough start in life, what with his ma dying when he was a babe and his ne'er-do-well father committing suicide when he was only fifteen. Didn't have much of a chance."

"Fifteen?" Bea said with a gasp. "Oh, I had not realised how young he was when it happened."

"It were bad, worse than you imagine. John told me—" Rachel paused at the sound of a knock.

"The carriage is waiting, my lady," one of the footmen said from the other side of the door.

"Very good, I shall be down directly," Bea called, frustrated by the interruption.

"I'll tell you the rest another time," Rachel said when Bea turned to her expectantly. "But I don't want you getting romantic notions about the man. Just because he was dealt a rough hand, ain't no reason to fall at his feet. He's an adult, and he's made his own bed. One which doesn't deserve you in it," she added, wagging a finger.

Bea rolled her eyes. "I'm not a fool, Rachel. I know very well what he is, and what he is not. I do not need warning, though it seems to me you have warmed towards him a good deal now your John has persuaded you he's not the devil."

"He's not *my* John," Rachel protested, flushing hotly, but happiness shone in her eyes.

"So you say," Bea retorted, smirking as she hurried from the room before Rachel could protest.

She smiled as she made her way down the stairs. So, that was how the wind blew, was it? How interesting. Perhaps she ought to find a bit more out about John. After all, Rachel, as tough as she might appear, was tender-hearted in truth. Bea did not wish to see her get her heart broken any more than she wished such a fate for herself.

"You're looking very grave, Beatrice, and very lovely too. That goes without saying."

Bea looked up and smiled as she saw Rutherford waiting for her. He looked so handsome this morning, his dark gold hair glinting in the bright daylight that filled the entrance hall. He wore fawn-coloured breeches with a superbly cut dark blue coat that showed off his physique marvellously well. His boots shone like glass and his deep blue eyes settled upon her, a smile lurking there.

"Good morning, my—Justin," she corrected herself, gaining a smile of delight at her remembering to use his name. "I beg your pardon, I was thinking about something I wish to discuss with you."

"Certainly. Shall we continue in the carriage or do you prefer to wait—"

"Oh, no. In the carriage. Let us go before I lose my nerve. I confess I am a little anxious," she admitted, which was something of an understatement.

Rutherford took her arm and escorted her outside, handing her up into the carriage. She noticed John and half a dozen footmen followed on horseback, making quite a procession.

"I would not, for one moment, take you anywhere near your uncle's house if I believed there was the slightest risk," he told her, his expression serious. Sitting down beside her, he reached for her hand, holding it in his. "I shan't let anyone upset you, certainly not hurt you. I give you my word."

Bea nodded, her heart thudding too hard at the feeling of his large hand holding hers, at the way he spoke so gravely, with such sincerity, his concern all for her, for her safety. *Oh, Bea, you are in a deal of trouble,* she thought ruefully.

Rather to her regret, Rutherford let go of her hand and sat back, regarding her with interest. "Now, then. What were you thinking so hard about as you came down the stairs?"

"I was thinking about John," she admitted.

"John? My valet?" he said, his brows tugging together. "Why?"

"I want to know a little about him. Is he a good man? Reliable? Do you trust him?"

He looked perplexed but considered her questions. "John is the best man I've ever known. He saved my life and stayed by my side when he had no reason to do so. He is the most honourable and trustworthy man of my acquaintance. I would say that John is more than my valet, he is my friend." He gazed at her curiously. "Might you explain to me why you ask such questions? I hope he is not under suspicion of wrongdoing?"

"Oh, no. Indeed, not. It's only..."

Bea hesitated. Everything Justin had told her was what she had hoped to hear, but she needed to know more. How did he treat women, would Rachel be safe with him? Yet, if she said anything, there was a risk Justin would pass the information on to John, that John might use it against Rachel if he were really not trustworthy. If she was to say anything to Justin, she must trust him to keep it to himself. She looked up at him, considering. *Yes*, her heart said, even as her mind told her she was a fool.

"Justin, if I tell you something in confidence, do you swear, upon your honour, to never speak a word of it to anyone else?"

He stilled, staring at her. For a moment she did not know what he would say, perhaps he would warn her not to trust him, the look in his eyes was so unreadable. Then he moved, reaching for her hand once more and holding on tight. "My Lady Rutherford. *Beatrice*, I swear you can put your trust in me. I promise I shall never speak a word, give a hint or write anything that breaks this vow, and… and I thank you for the opportunity to prove myself to you. My honour is not something anyone has asked me for in a very, very long time, but it means everything to me that you would do so."

Bea let out a breath, startled by the intensity of his reply. She hadn't anticipated his reaction, nor understood what it might signify to a man branded as dishonourable.

"I beg your pardon, I have startled you," he said ruefully, removing his hand from hers.

Impulsively, Bea's fingers tightened, holding onto him. "No, I… I am glad, and I believe you."

He smiled at that, looking almost bashful but pleased by her words. "Well then, what is this great secret?"

Bea returned his smile. "I may be completely wrong, you understand, but I believe there may be a romance blooming under our noses."

"Ah, now it makes sense," he replied, nodding. "You speak of John and Rachel?"

"Yes!" she exclaimed, turning in her seat to face him. "Oh, you devil. You let me run on and all the time you knew."

"I didn't know that's what you wished to speak of!" he protested. "Truly, I did not, but are you telling me that Rachel reciprocates? I beg you will get her to give the poor fellow a hint if she does, for he's been moping about like a lovesick hound for days now. It's appalling."

Bea gave a bark of laughter, which made him grin. "Oh, you wicked man. How can you speak so of your friend?"

"I speak so because he is my friend," he replied frankly. "And I must ask, I suppose, as you represent Rachel, I must do so for my dear John."

"She is an angel," Bea said firmly, understanding at once, and then she hesitated. "Well, maybe not an *angel*. She's not one to suffer fools, I'll give you that, but she is patient and kind and loyal and brave and I do not know what I should have done without her. She was a true friend when I was alone and desperate. I shall never be able to repay her for that, but I am trying," she added, for she had raised Rachel's wages so much she was likely the best paid lady's maid in the country.

"It sounds as if they are well suited, then," Justin suggested.

Bea nodded. "I think so. I certainly hope so. Wouldn't it be lovely if a romance bloomed out of a situation that was so desperately awful?"

Justin's hand squeezed her fingers. "It would," he said, his voice soft.

Bea looked up at him, her heart giving an uneven thud as she saw the warmth in his eyes, the wistful glint there that she dared not believe in. Not yet. Maybe never.

"Oh, this is the driveway," she said, sitting up and tugging her hand from his. "We're here."

❄ ❄ ❄ ❄ ❄

Justin cursed the driver's wretched timing. If only he'd had a few more minutes, perhaps he might have found the words he'd needed to tell her what was in his heart. Not that she would have believed him, he thought darkly. Not if she had any sense. He wondered how long it would take to prove to her he had changed, that *she* had changed him. Years and years and years. The answer made his spirits plummet when they had soared just moments before. Buck up, he told himself. She had trusted him, trusted him enough to ask him to keep his word, and believed that he *would* keep it. That was more than he had ever expected a few short weeks ago. It was progress, and he would keep making progress, no matter how slow it was, no matter how long it took, even if it was the years and years and years he feared it might be.

Her uncle's house was a modern red brick building of elegant proportions but was modest when compared to Chalfont House. No wonder the fortune his older brother had amassed had rankled so. He must have coveted it for decades and assumed he would gain more control when his brother died. To have his niece thwart him so thoroughly must stick in his throat like a bramble thorn. Good, Justin thought with satisfaction. He hoped the bastard choked on it.

He stepped out, reaching a hand back to help Beatrice rather than letting the footman do it. Justin was not about to miss an opportunity to take her hand, and once she had stepped down, he tucked it carefully into the crook of his arm. He looked at John, who had dismounted and come to stand beside them.

"If we're not out in fifteen minutes, you'd best make a fuss and demand to see us."

"With pleasure, my lord," John replied with a grin.

Justin nodded and turned back to Beatrice.

"Ready, love?" he asked her, realising too late he had spoken an endearment when he had promised to behave as a brother to her.

She did not seem to notice; the colour had drained from her face, and she looked pale. He thought perhaps she was trembling.

"You do not need to do this," he said, keeping his voice low. "You may remain in the carriage and simply issue instructions if—"

"No." She shook her head, putting up her chin. "I am ready. I can do this, if… if you remain by my side, I can do this."

"I'm going nowhere," he promised her, wishing she understood that the promise was for more than just this moment, this day.

She nodded. "Very well, then."

He guided her up the path to the front door, and Justin knocked.

The door swung open, and the butler's eyes widened as he recognised them. "Miss Huntingdon," he said in shock.

"That's my Lady Rutherford to you," Justin said coldly, determined that everyone in the damned house understand that the Countess of Rutherford deserved the full measure of respect such a title was due. Her husband might be a wastrel, but she was everything a lady ought to be and should be treated as such.

"My lady, my lord," the butler corrected hastily. "If you would come this way, I shall see if Lord Worth is at home."

They followed the butler through to a small parlour. No fire was burning, and the room was on the north side of the house, making it dark and rather gloomy.

"I had forgotten what an oppressive atmosphere there is here," Bea said, clutching her arms about herself. "I hated it here, Justin. I was utterly wretched."

Justin moved to stand beside her, resting his hand at the small of her back, hoping she would see it as the comforting gesture he meant it to be. She did not move away, even leaning into his touch a little. "That's over now. We shall collect the things you wish to take and go home."

Home.

The word resonated like the last note of a concerto, ringing long after it had first sounded. It reverberated in his heart, warming him. His house, the place where he had been born and raised, had never been his home. It had been the place he'd lived in when he wasn't at school, or when he had disgraced himself sufficiently that he must hide from society. But it had never been home. It was now, because she was there, because she had made it a home for him.

She nodded, turning to gaze up at him, a tentative smile on her lips. "That's a happy thought," she said, as if the word had struck her too, meaning more than the property they dwelled in together.

The door flew open, and she jolted as her uncle stood before them. His expression was one of utter disbelief.

"You dare?" he said in outrage. "You dare come here? What is it you want?"

"Only those things that belong to my wife," Justin said, reaching for Beatrice's hand and holding it tightly. "We will not stay above a moment, but you have no right to keep her from collecting them."

"I've thrown them out," her uncle said with a sneer. "We burnt everything."

Justin snorted, the man was clearly lying, blustering and hoping to hurt Beatrice with his words. She clung to him, holding on as though he offered a lifeline. "Well, which is it? Did you burn them or throw them out? Perhaps we shall just check to be certain nothing remains. My lady," he said, glancing down at Beatrice.

Her face was ashen, her lips tight, but she nodded at him.

Justin walked towards the door, but Lord Worth did not move. "I should hate to have to knock you down in your own home," Justin said silkily. "But I shall."

The man glared at him, so furious his face burned, his eyes bulging in a manner that could not be good for his health. Still, he stepped aside, and Justin guided Beatrice up the stairs.

"It's this way," she said, moving along the hall until she reached the room that had been hers. She hurried inside and then turned to give him a dazzling smile. "He was lying!" she said, beaming at him.

Justin's heart lurched. Christ, he was in a bad way, but he would have dismantled her uncle's house brick by brick if she asked it of him, if he could only be worthy of another smile like that one.

He watched as she pulled a small trunk out from under the bed and rushed about, filling it with books and pictures, and her treasured possessions. Pulling open the doors of a large wardrobe, she got to her knees and buried herself under the gowns. A folded blanket, a pillow and several folded petticoats were thrown behind her, before she reached to the far back and tugged.

"Do you need help?" Justin asked, moving to crouch beside her, curious to know what she was doing.

"No... I've... I've got it," she said, her voice muffled as she drew a small but apparently heavy chest out. It thudded as she dragged it from the wardrobe, out onto the floor. "My jewellery," she said in triumph.

"There's a lot?" Justin suggested, for the chest was solid, banded around with iron and with a hefty lock. You did not take such precautions if there were only a few trinkets inside.

Bea nodded. "Papa spoiled me. I told my uncle he did not approve of jewellery, that he thought it vulgar, and I hid the trunk in Rachel's belongings when we came here. I never really trusted him, you see. Papa thought Uncle Charles was vulgar, and Charles knew it, so he believed me, I think. He must have done, for if he'd known it was here, he would have taken it."

"Clever girl," Justin said approvingly.

Bea flushed but looked pleased by the comment.

"Well, that's everything."

"You do not wish to take the gowns?" he asked, gesturing to the wardrobe which was full.

"No," she said firmly. "They're all mourning gowns and I have no desire to be reminded of such an unhappy time in my life."

Justin nodded and took the chest, placing it inside the larger one she had dragged from under the bed. Closing it securely, he tested the weight. It was heavy, but he could manage it. He did not trust her uncle to let them back in again if he went to fetch John, and he was not about to leave her alone in this place.

"Beatrice!"

The feminine voice was an exclamation of shock and John turned to see a woman of about his wife's age standing just inside the room. He supposed she was pretty, in an obvious sort of way. She had the same fine build as Beatrice, but her features were a little too sharp, her mouth one that looked like it turned down more often than it turned up. Her hair was blonde, fine, thin ringlets hanging around her heart-shaped face.

"I cannot believe you dare to come back here after what you did!" the young woman said, her cheeks flushed. "And… And to bring *him*."

Beatrice stiffened at her words, her green eyes flashing with anger. "Ah, yes, Dorothy, I forgot you have not met my husband. May I present the Earl of Rutherford?"

"I know who he is," Dorothy spat. "Everyone knows who he is. He is a disgrace and not fit to be in the same room as a lady."

"Then you had better flee before he eats you," Beatrice suggested sweetly.

Justin choked back a laugh, not entirely successfully, for Dorothy glared at him and then once more at Beatrice. "Papa told me what you did, that you'd been carrying on with him all the time you were here. It's disgusting. No wonder you spoke kindly of him when Rogers told us he was going to die from his wounds. He was already your lover."

"Is that what he said?" Beatrice said, her eyes going wide at the accusation. "Good lord, Dorothy, and you believed him, you little peewit. How exactly did I get out of my room and all the way to Chalfont House, make love to Lord Rutherford, and then come home again, all without anyone noticing, pray tell? You might remember I hardly had a moment alone, for you were with me most all the time. Whether I liked it or not," she added indignantly.

Justin decided he loved her all the more for that little bit of spite, which he did not doubt Dorothy thoroughly deserved. That Bea had also spoken kindly of him before they had even met was something that warmed his soul.

Dorothy hesitated.

Beatrice stepped forward. "Do you remember the day I disappeared? Do you remember how all the servants had gone? Do you remember Mr Runcible?"

Dorothy made a face of disgust. "That vile creature. I cannot think why Papa invited him. He made me most uncomfortable, and why all the servants must take leave on the same day, I never understood," she added frankly. "It was most inconvenient when I needed my belongings packed to return to town."

"Your Papa had decided I was to marry Mr Runcible, and when I refused, he told me he would lock me in my room and that Mr Runcible alone would have the key. Then Uncle Charles was going to leave with you, so only Mr Runcible and I would be here, with no servants. Mr Runcible was going to persuade me to marry him, Dorothy. Do you understand how he was going to do that?"

To her credit, Dorothy turned a ghastly shade of green, her hand going to her throat. Beatrice leaned in, whispering to her. "I should choose a husband and get married as fast as you can, Dorothy, for perhaps your Papa might find a Mr Runcible for you, one who is rich and old, or weak enough for him to manipulate."

Dorothy gasped, shaking her head. "I don't… Oh, Beatrice. I don't want that."

"No, and neither did I!" Beatrice told her, gripping her arms. "Now listen to me, Dorothy, and listen well. You have a care with your papa, but if you ever need my help, you write to me, and I shall come. Or you come to Chalfont House, and I shall help you however I can. Do you understand?"

Dorothy burst into tears, and Beatrice sighed, pulling her into a hug. "There, there. Your papa loves you far more than he ever did me. He never even liked me, Dot, you know that. He only ever wanted my father's money. Don't be frightened now, but do be careful, and remember what I said."

"I sh-shall." Dorothy gave a weak sniff. "And I'm s-sorry for the wicked things I said about you. I never stopped to think about how impossible it was. I shan't ever say them again, and I shall tell people they are wrong if I hear such things said too," she added stoutly.

"Thank you, Dorothy," Beatrice said, patting her hand. "Now, if you will excuse us, I would like to leave before your father gets any notions about keeping us here."

Dorothy nodded and watched as Justin hefted the heavy chest and they walked down the stairs. She did not follow. Justin did not doubt she wanted no part in any further confrontation with her father. He could not blame her.

The butler ran from the front hall as he spied them on their way down and Justin sighed inwardly, certain Lord Worth had told the man to alert him when they were ready to go.

As he had anticipated, Lord Worth slammed out of a room, the crash of the door echoing from somewhere in the house in the moments before he appeared.

"Get out of my house, you little slut, and don't ever think of returning again."

He spat the words at Beatrice and Justin did not think, only reacted. He set the chest down before turning on the man, grabbing hold of his coat lapels and propelling him back against the nearest surface. He heard Worth's head hit the wall and felt nothing but grim satisfaction.

"Apologise," he growled, low in his throat, the desire to smash his fist into the bastard's face so tantalising he was vibrating with it.

"Let go of me. Petersham, help me, damn you!" he called, trying to summon the butler.

Justin turned a volcanic glare upon the man, who had taken a hesitant step forward. "Try it," he suggested.

Petersham thought better of his choices and didn't move.

Justin adjusted his grip, taking hold of the man's neckcloth and twisting. "Apologise, or I'll choke the life from you, just see if I don't."

Worth made a spluttering sound, and Justin released his grip enough for him to speak.

"Sorry," he spat out, glaring furiously at Justin, hands scrabbling to no avail, trying to loosen his hold.

"Not to me, to her, you cretin," Justin bellowed, giving the man a shake that must have rattled his teeth. "You will say, 'I am sorry, my Lady Rutherford.'"

"S-Sorry, my Lady R-Rutherford," Worth managed, though his eyes blazed with rage.

"Sweetheart?" Justin called over his shoulder.

"I heard, thank you, Justin. You may let him go," Beatrice said coolly.

Justin did, stepping back as her uncle slid down the wall, sitting on the marble floor with a thud, panting. Beatrice came to stand beside him and took his arm, gazing down at her uncle with disgust.

"I do not forgive you, Uncle Charles. I never shall. Come, Justin, take me home, please."

"With pleasure, love," Justin said, smiling at her. They walked to the door, arm—in—arm. Justin opened it, calling for John to come and take the chest. He accompanied Beatrice outside and helped her into the carriage. Justin watched her anxiously, but she said nothing until they were halfway up the drive.

"Justin?" Her voice was quiet, a little unsteady, and he turned, wondering if she was angry with him for what he'd done.

"Yes?"

She gave a choked sob and threw herself against his chest. For a moment he was too stunned to move, to accept that she was turning to him for comfort, but then his scattered wits returned to him, and he put his arms around her, holding on tight.

"There, there, darling girl. Don't upset yourself. He's a wicked man. An unhappy, wicked man who does not understand what it is to love or be loved. You must pity him if you feel anything at all. Do not dwell on it, do not let the past taint the future, for that is the biggest mistake you will ever make. Take it from one who knows, love. As far as we understand, we only get one life, and there is too little time to throw any of it away on revenge or regret or dwelling on the past. Look to your future now. You won, and you're the better person, a kind and clever, lovely and wonderful person," he added, his own voice growing a little unsteady as he spoke.

Beatrice stilled, sniffing, and Justin searched his coat anxiously, making a mental note to thank John when he discovered a pristine white handkerchief. He handed it to her, and she wiped her eyes, giving her nose a very unladylike blow that made him smile.

"I beg your pardon," she said thickly. "I did not mean to weep all over you."

"I rather enjoyed it," he admitted, hurrying to qualify the remark as she gave him an odd look. "Not that you were upset and crying, only—only that you turned to me. I am glad you turned to me. I only want to do that for you, Beatrice. I shall always be here, to chase problems away, to offer clean handkerchiefs, to strangle obnoxious men or… or just to offer moral support. If you will allow it." He watched her anxiously, hoping he'd not ruined everything by making an ill-considered remark.

Her mouth turned up at the corners. "I hope I shall not need you to strangle anyone else. At least, not for a day or two."

Justin gave a bark of laughter, delighted by her. "You just let me know, eh?"

She nodded, sniffing, but it seemed the storm had passed, and she was in control once more.

"Do you really think your cousin will put people straight if they speak ill of us?" he asked, curious about what she really thought of Dorothy. Justin considered himself a fair judge of character and, personally, he would not trust the girl an inch.

"Of course not," Beatrice said with a laugh. "Dorothy has no backbone, the poor dear. She will agree with whomever she speaks with and then contradict herself if the next person disagrees. It is only that she wishes to be liked so desperately, but of course it becomes impossible when one realises she is never sincere, even though she may believe what she says when she says it. She is not a bad person, only a weak one."

Justin nodded, having surmised as much. "Do you mind very much that people are gossiping about you, about us?" he asked quietly. He had never before wished to undo everything he had done wrong in his life so much as he did now. It had been many years since he had enjoyed his dreadful behaviour, if indeed he ever had. Looking back, he was not sure it had ever brought him anything close to happiness.

To his surprise, she shook her head. "Not at the moment. I suppose I will if I ever go to town. If people stare and point and cut me in the street, I may mind very much indeed, but I shall never regret my decision, Justin." She turned to look at him and Justin's breath caught as he gazed into her lovely green eyes, wishing he were worthy of the woman beside him. "I wish you to know that," she added, her voice firm.

Justin swallowed, his throat absurdly tight. "Beatrice, if I could change it, change the past, every bit of it, I would do so," he said, hoping she could hear how desperately he meant the words.

"If wishes were horses, beggars would ride," she said with a wry smile. "A wise man once told me not to waste time on regrets."

Justin laughed, nodding. "Not so wise as all that, I fear."

"Wise enough," she said with a smile, and they made their way home together.

Chapter 9

"Wherein the past is stirred up."

25th November 1820.

Bea moved through the huge attic room, hugging her shawl tighter around her. It was freezing up here, but they had found a few treasures she was so delighted with, it was worth the time in the cold.

"There are paintings over here, my lady," Rachel called. "Oh, come and look. This must be your husband's mama."

Bea hurried over to where Rachel was uncovering a stack of paintings, hefting a dusty Holland cover aside.

"Oh," Bea said, her hand covering her heart as she looked at the lovely portrait. The woman was beautiful, and so very young, making her shiver with some emotion she could not decipher.

"Oh, and this must be his father," Rachel exclaimed. "Look! I'd think it were him if not for the style of his clothes."

Bea turned, gasping as she saw what Rachel meant. The man was handsome, with a wicked glint of amusement in his dark blue eyes, his lips curved upwards a little, as if he knew a splendid joke and was only waiting for the right moment to share it with you.

"Shall we take them down?" Rachel asked, admiring the portraits. "They'd look lovely downstairs in your parlour."

Bea nodded, for Rachel was right. "They would, but I shan't put them up yet. I think I had better ask Rutherford first. They are probably up here for a reason. I do not wish to cause him any unhappiness if seeing them causes him pain. You said Justin was fifteen when he killed himself?" Bea asked, reaching out to touch the painting of his father.

The painting was so exquisitely done that Bea felt she could really touch the softness of his golden hair, a little surprised when her fingers met canvas and cold paint.

"Yes, that's right. Bankrupt he was, debts up to his ears. He weren't much older than Rutherford is now, I reckon. His lordship, your husband that is, took it hard, from what John said."

Bea considered what it must have been like to have no memory of his mother, and then for his father to desert him, leaving him burdened with debts he could never pay.

"Leave them here," she said suddenly. "I must speak with Rutherford first. If he wishes them to remain here, then they shall."

"Very well," Rachel said with a shrug. "What about this? It's pretty."

Bea nodded as she regarded the little landscape of horses against a wintery sky. "Yes, that can come down, and the chairs we found. I think that's all for now, Rachel, we'll look at the others another day. I'm frozen and I'm sure you must be too. I think it's time for tea."

Rachel nodded, as eager as Bea to escape the cold.

Bea made her way downstairs, pleased to enter her parlour and find a cheery fire blazing. She stood with her hands outstretched for a moment before she heard voices outside in the garden. Curious, Bea went to the window and looked out, smiling as she watched Justin in conversation with one of the workmen. The man nodded and tugged his cap before striding off and Justin looked up at the house. Bea raised her hand, waving at him.

Her heart gave a silly little skip in her heart as he mirrored her action, waving back. Impulsively, Bea gestured to him, telling him to come.

His grin widened, and he saluted her smartly before he walked around the house, making her laugh. Bea returned to her position by the fire as she waited for him, warming her hands, her pulse suddenly rapid at the notion she would see him any moment. Foolishness, she told herself. They breakfasted together most every morning and dined three times a week, too. Justin had kept his word and was a charming companion, one she delighted in, and trusted too, for he never flirted or pushed for more than she had offered him.

She had wondered if perhaps he did not see her as a woman any longer, if perhaps he did not find her alluring and so it was easy to act as though she were indeed his sister. But then she would catch a look in his eyes, something hot and dark that would make her stomach clench and her heart thud as her nerves ran riot. Not that he ever acted upon those hungry looks.

On the nights when she didn't eat with him, Bea took her meals in her room, and with each day that passed, she hated those lonely evenings more. Tonight was one of those nights, when she would have to eat alone, without his lively conversation, without the pleasure of his company.

The door opened, and Bea smiled as Justin came in, crossing the room towards her.

"My lady," he said, bowing formally, though a twinkle lurked in his eyes. "You commanded my presence."

"Did I?" Bea said, laughing. "I beg your pardon, I did not mean to do so. I only thought you looked cold and wondered if you might like to take tea with me."

An expression of genuine pleasure crossed his face. "I should be delighted to. Thank you."

Bea nodded, captured by the look in his eyes. She could not look away, caught in the deep blue of his gaze, and found herself swallowing anxiously. The door opened and Bea let out a breath, relieved as a footman carried in the tea tray. He set it down on the table beside Bea's chair and she dismissed the man, settling herself down.

Justin sat opposite her, reclining elegantly as always, his gaze still resting upon her. She could feel the weight of it, feel the warmth of it against her skin as tangibly as she could feel the heat of the fire.

Bea prepared Justin's tea the way he liked it, lifting the cup as he got to his feet to accept it. "There's cake too, and biscuits," she said, gesturing to the tray where a sugar dusted jam sponge sat beside a plate piled high with butter biscuits.

"Cake, please," Justin said. "I have a sweet tooth."

"I know, I prepared your tea," she said, smiling at him. "Two lumps in that little cup," she scolded, shaking her head.

He laughed at that and returned a rueful shrug. "I know, I know, and you take none because you are sweet enough."

"Not so sweet that I shall forgo the cake," she remarked tartly, cutting them both a generous slice. "We shall make the Christmas cake tomorrow after church. Will you come and stir up with us?"

He gave her a quizzical look as he accepted the slice of cake. "Stir up?"

Bea gazed at him in astonishment. "It's Stir Up Sunday," she said, assuming this would clarify things for him. Apparently not, as the blank gaze remained. "Good heavens. You've never stirred a Christmas cake before?"

"Er… no?" he replied, obviously bemused as he took a bite of the cake, chewing with pleasure, judging from his expression.

Bea shook her head, and then remembered his mother died when he was a baby, and whilst she did not know what his father had been like, she assumed he'd not been one for domesticity. The man in the portrait had looked like a handsome rake, just like his son.

"It's tradition," she said, taking a sip of her tea. "On the last Sunday before Advent, you make the mixture for Christmas cakes and puddings. The family all come together and stir the mixture from east to west, to represent the journey the wise men took on their way to visit the baby Jesus. It brings good luck for the coming year."

He was watching her, an oddly wistful gleam in his eyes. "And… you would like me to come and stir up with you?" He looked away, chasing the last crumbs of the cake around his plate with a fingertip.

There was something in his voice too, a careful quality, as if he didn't trust the invitation or perhaps that he was afraid of finding it wasn't real. Bea considered his question, considered if the invitation was offering him more than the simple act of stirring a pudding.

"Yes, I would," she replied firmly, heart thudding.

He looked up and his smile did the most peculiar thing to her stupid, stupid heart.

"Then I shall be in the kitchen at the appointed hour. Only tell me when, and if I must dress for the occasion," he said mischievously.

She laughed at that. "Well, it's clearly a formal occasion," she teased him. "Evening dress is a must."

He nodded, as if he took her words seriously, though laughter shone in the blue depths of his gaze. "I thought as much."

Bea smiled at him, a warm sensation in her chest, something very much like hope. She tried to squash it down, tried to tell herself she did not, could not, trust it, but the sensation lingered all the same. It diminished only when she remembered the portraits, and what she had intended to ask him. Her thoughts must have shown on her face.

"What is it? Have you decided to rescind the invitation so soon?" he asked, only half joking, she thought.

Bea shook her head. "No. I beg your pardon, it's only—"

She took a breath, steeling her nerve and praying he would not be angry with her. It was such a pleasant interlude, this time with him, and she did not wish to spoil it. Perhaps she ought to ask him another time.

"It's only?" he prompted.

Bea sighed. "Do you promise not to be cross with me?"

His lips quirked. "Whom have you murdered, little Boudicca?"

"No one!" she replied, huffing at him. "It's nothing like that. It's only I found some things in the attic, and I would very much like to bring them down, but I shall not, if you prefer I leave them alone."

"Why should I mind?" he asked in confusion.

"Because they're portraits of your parents."

He blinked at her, and for a moment she wondered if he had heard her words. Then he let out a breath. "I see."

He set his empty plate aside and got to his feet, walking to the window.

"I'm sorry. I ought not to have asked," she said wretchedly, cursing herself for having spoken of a subject that was bound to be painful to him.

He turned, shaking his head before looking outside again. One hand lifted to the back of his neck and squeezed. "No. No do not be sorry. It's only that you took me by surprise. I'd half-forgotten they were there."

"Only half?" she asked softly.

He shrugged, still not looking at her. "Such memories are never buried that deeply, I suppose, no matter how one tries."

"They are a very handsome couple," she offered, hoping to lighten the moment.

Justin nodded. "My mother died before I knew her, but that portrait was always in this room, over there," he said, gesturing to the spot on the wall where Bea had instinctively thought to hang the picture. "I did not know who she was until I was perhaps six years old, and my nanny told me."

"Your father didn't—"

Justin let out a breath of laughter. "My father could not bear to be in the house once my mother had gone. It was the one thing that comforted me as a lad, that they had loved each other when they made me. When she died, I believe he went a little mad. He certainly did not remember he had a son."

"You never saw him?"

He shook his head. "No. But I became obsessed with the portrait, and I would sit before it for hours and hours, gazing at my mother, wondering if I had been a very bad child for her not to want to stay with me."

Bea's heart clenched at the words, but he turned around to face her before she could say anything foolish. "Of course, Nanny told me it was no such thing. That her death was nothing to do with me at all, that she had been ill and had died. But she said that she did not hold with such mawkish sentimentality. So she took the portrait down and had it sent to the attic."

"You've not seen it since?" Bea asked.

He shook his head. "No. I think I should like to, though, so I thank you for finding it."

Bea let out a breath of relief and then realised he had not said if his father's portrait was also welcome.

"And… And the other one?"

He did not answer for a long time. "My father," he began and then shook his head. "I do not know."

"He's very like you," she offered, and then wished the words unsaid as he swung around, his eyes blazing with emotion.

"Oh, very like," he agreed, his tone one she did not like, full of self-loathing. "Two peas in a pod."

"Don't say that," she snapped at him, suddenly angry for reasons she was not entirely certain of.

He stilled, frowning at her. "Why not? It's what everyone else in the world says. Cut from the same cloth, following the same path to destruction."

"Because you are not your father, because you are not bankrupt and have not run out of choices."

His fists clenched, and he turned away, his shoulders rigid. "If I am not bankrupt, that is because of you and nothing *I* ever did, but my father had choices, too. There were still properties to sell, land, but he left that all to me to do. He cared nothing but for his own pain and embarrassment, the loss of his honour was more important than I was, he left me alone with the wolves circling."

There was such anger behind the words, such rage and pain, that Bea hesitated. Perhaps she should leave him alone to calm down, it was not her place to comfort him and… and yet whose place was it if not his wife's, his friend's?

She got to her feet and crossed to him, hardly knowing how she dared as she reached out and took his hand, curling her fingers about his. Words crowded on her tongue, but she did not know if they were the right ones, the ones that would help ease the hurt, but she had to try, had to say *something*.

"He left those properties and that land for you, so you would not be so encumbered once he was gone. Perhaps he believed he was doing it for the best, that you would be better off without him.

I know he would have wanted to see you grow, to have been beside you, but perhaps he did not feel worthy of that. I cannot imagine how disordered a man's mind must be to believe he has no other option but to end his life, but I do not believe he would have done it to hurt you, Justin, perhaps he did it to save you, to help you make better choices."

Justin swung around, staring at her with such shock in his eyes that she took a step back. He was breathing hard, like the air had been knocked from his lungs.

"Justin, I'm sorry," Bea exclaimed, appalled that she had been so clumsy, that she had said something to hurt or shock him so profoundly.

"Excuse me," he said, his voice hoarse, before he let go of her hand and hurried from the room.

Justin fled the house without coat or hat, hurrying outside and sucking in deep lungfuls of air. Bea's gentle voice, filled with such empathy and understanding, filled his ears, the things she had said echoing over and over, tenderly destroying everything he had believed of his father, everything he had told himself for decades, with a few well-chosen words.

Good luck, son. I pray you do better than I did.

Justin hurried away from the house, across the gardens, out into the trees, walking until he found himself in the middle of the woodland that surrounded much of Chalfont. Trees towered overhead, skeletal branches hung with the occasional dead leaf as their fallen brethren crunched underfoot.

He left those properties and that land for you, so you would not be so encumbered once he was gone. Perhaps he believed he was doing it for the best, that you would be better off without him.

He leaned back against the trunk of an immense oak tree, one that would not have been noticeably smaller when his father had been a boy.

I pray you do better than I did.

But he hadn't done better, had he? He'd not understood what his father had been trying to tell him, what Bea had explained without hesitation. Instead, he'd been worse, done worse, fallen far farther than his father ever had.

"No," he said shakily. "No."

Because he wasn't dead yet. He wasn't bankrupt thanks to his wife, and though his honour might be beyond salvage in the eyes of the *ton*, Beatrice did not look at him with contempt. For reasons he did not understand, she had offered him friendship despite knowing from the outset that he was a bad bet. She had told him so at that very first meeting, had she not, told him they ought to live separate lives, and yet she had softened towards him, seen something in him worthy of trust, worthy of her time. If she could still find something good in him, some remnant of the man he might have been, then surely it was not too late.

He would make sure it was not too late.

Chapter 10

"Wherein the festive season weaves a little magic."

26th November 1820.

"You still going to church in the village, then?" Rachel asked sceptically as she helped Bea dress the next morning.

Bea nodded. She needed forgiveness for her stupidity the day before, and facing the gossip and whispers from her neighbours would be an act of penance. Until now, she had visited the tiny chapel on the estate on Sunday mornings, spending a few quiet moments in solitude before lighting a candle for her father. She had always meant to gather her courage and visit the church in Tenterden, but now it seemed something she *must* do in repentance for her hubris.

She had thought to ease the feelings that Justin had lived with for most of his life, but clearly, she had only hurt him and made things far worse. Her stomach roiled as she remembered the shock in his eyes. Rachel had it from John that he had not come home until after dark, despite the bitter temperature and the fact he had gone out with neither coat nor hat. She prayed he had not caught a chill.

"Well, I'll send word to the stables, then," Rachel said, gathering the dirty linens and bustling to the door. "Unless there's anything else?"

"No, thank you, Rachel," Bea said, giving her a wan smile before she sat at her dressing table. As she stared into the looking glass, her reflection showed a woman who had slept ill, filled with guilt and regret. Sighing, Bea pinched her cheeks hard and bit her lips, trying to gain a little colour. Then she selected a pair of diamond and pearl earbobs, attaching them carefully before considering the results. If people were going to stare at her, she would give them no reason to find fault with Rutherford's new countess.

She made her way down the stairs, smiling at Morley as he greeted her.

"Good morning, my lady. It's a fine bright day, but bitter cold."

Bea nodded. "Thank you for the warning. I shall take my warmest cloak, if you would fetch it for me, please?"

Morley nodded, gesturing for a footman who hurried away. "I took the liberty of ordering a hot brick and told the footman to get it warmed again at the pub while he waited for you for the journey home."

"Why, how thoughtful, Morley, thank you," Bea said, touched by the man's kindness.

Morley's face lit up, a tinge of colour cresting his cheeks. "It is my pleasure," he assured her, taking her cloak from the footman and settling it upon her shoulders.

Bea accepted her bonnet from the footman and stood before the mirror to tie the ribbons. Movement behind her caught her eye, and she startled as she saw Rutherford in the reflection. She spun around and then realised she could say nothing with Morley and the footmen present. So she just stood, gazing at him stupidly and hoping he knew how sorry she was.

Justin smiled at her and her heart eased a little, for there seemed to be no anger, no condemnation in his gaze. "I understand you are going to church in Tenterden this morning. Would you mind very much if I accompanied you? I shall understand if you prefer—"

"No!" Bea exclaimed, so loudly she winced. "No, my lord, I should be glad, *very glad*, for your company."

Justin inclined his head, offering his arm and Bea took it, hoping he was only waiting, as she was, for them to be alone in the carriage before he said what was on his mind.

Justin escorted her out, handing her up into the carriage with all the solicitude he always showed her, and soon they were sitting side-by-side. The carriage moved off. Bea took a deep breath, and the words exploded from her.

"Justin, I'm so sorry, I had no right—"

"I pray you will forgive me—"

They both spoke at once and then stared at each other in bemusement.

"Forgive you for what?"

"What are you sorry for?"

Having done it a second time, they both laughed, realising how ridiculous they were being.

"Let me go first," Bea begged him, getting the words out before he could. "I've been awake all night, regretting ever having mentioned those portraits, for having stirred up memories I ought to have realised could be nothing but painful, and then for my own conceit in believing I could ever say anything to ease that pain."

"But you did," Justin replied, stunning her into silence.

"I-I did?"

Justin was quiet for a long moment, but then he reached for her hand, lacing their fingers together. "Do you mind?" he asked, carrying on when she shook her head. "There is something about you that steadies me, that makes me feel as if I am rooted somehow. I imagine that sounds foolish to you, but I have spent my life feeling as if I drifted like a leaf on the breeze, going where fate blew me. I believe, now that I have taken the time to consider such things, that I assumed if I left my fate in the hands of chance, the things that happened were not really my fault at all. The reasoning of a boy, I fear. A stupid, stupid boy."

Bea held her tongue, determined not to make the same mistake again, though she longed to comfort him, even to make excuses for him when she had no right to do so. He had been appalling. If even half the stories about his behaviour were true, he deserved much of what had befallen him, and yet she still wished to protect him from it. In that moment, she realised just how hard was falling for him. Though she did not know exactly when or even why it had happened, she had made the fatal mistake of falling in love with her husband. He had the power to hurt her now, the power to make her utterly wretched, and yet with his large hand holding hers so warmly, she could not regret it. Not yet, at least.

"I told you my mother died when I was a baby and that I did not know my father, save for occasional glimpses of him. Well, he came home once. It was the summer holidays of the year I turned fifteen. He spent the entire summer with me. All day, every day, and I had never been happier. We were friends, I thought, and I knew no father in the world had ever been better than my own. We talked, and he spent the days teaching me everything he knew, some things I certainly needed to know, others that he ought never to have shown me, but I did not know, did not understand, that he was preparing me for a life he would never again play a part in. I was wretched when I returned to school, counting the days until the next holiday where I assumed I would see him again, for we were such great friends now, he could not possibly wish to be anywhere but by my side… so reasoned my fifteen-year-old self," he said with a sorrowful smile.

Bea's heart clenched, guessing what came next.

"I got the news two weeks later and was promptly ejected from school because the bill had not been paid in months and now never would be."

"Justin," Bea said helplessly, squeezing his fingers tightly but too afraid to utter words of sympathy, even though they burned in her throat and made tears prick at her eyes.

"The last thing my father said to me," Justin said, his voice calm, almost peaceful as he returned the squeeze of her fingers, "was 'Good luck, son. I pray you do better than I did.' I did not realise at the time that he really meant it, that he prayed I would be better, happier than he had been."

"I'm… I'm so sorry," Beatrice said, because she couldn't *not* say it, couldn't let him believe she was unmoved by his words when her heart was breaking for him.

"Beatrice, I've made a mess of everything," he said, his head turned away from her, his gaze fixed on some distant place she could not see. "I set out to outdo my father. For I knew he was the best man in the world, I admired and loved him so fiercely in the childish manner of a boy worshiping a god. I would hear no criticism of him, and if I heard stories of his wickedness, I would seek to outdo him, so no one could think ill of him, for his son was far worse." He shook his head and gave an unhappy huff of laughter.

"You were grieving," Bea said, her voice unsteady. "Was there no one to offer you comfort?"

"Only mad old Aunt Sophronia, who told me I was a hell-born babe and would join my father soon enough. At the time, I prayed she was right. Other than that, a few servants remained, the ones I could afford to keep after paying off all my father's debts."

Bea tried to imagine what that must have been like for a grieving boy, alone in that great house, with only a few servants for company.

"My father had taught me to gamble that summer, and so began my career of wickedness," he said, shaking his head. "By the time I was eighteen, I had won and lost another fortune, fought my first duel over a woman, and sunk so far that I knew I would never see the light again. And I didn't. Not for years and years. Not until the night you walked into my life."

Bea's breath caught at his words, and she blinked, stunned, hardly able to believe she had heard them correctly. Had he really said that? Had he really meant that? But the carriage had pulled up beside the church where a throng of people gathered, starting to make their way inside.

A footman opened the door and Justin got out before she could stop him, before she could find something to say in reply. Then his hand was reaching for hers and she looked down into eyes of such blue, eyes that for once held no glimmer of a smile or wickedness. He looked tired, as though he were searching for something in her.

Bea held his gaze and took his hand, not looking away as she stepped down from the carriage. "Thank you," she said, and hoped he understood she was thanking him for more than the simple act he'd performed.

Tension thrummed between them as she put her hand on his arm and Bea wished they did not need to go inside the church. She did not wish to break the spell that seemed to have been cast over them, the sense of intimacy she did not wish to lose but feared would vanish like a soap bubble if anyone else broke into their world.

Her fears were realised as she overheard whispers behind them. Bea stiffened as she heard the words—*rake, libertine, no better than she ought to be.*

"Ignore them," Justin told her, placing his hand atop hers. "They know nothing of us nor our lives and, whatever the truth or the lies they speak, we should not care for them. It's none of our business what they think or say, so we shall not let it trouble us."

Bea opened her mouth to protest, to say that it was not that easy, but suddenly, staring into his eyes and seeing the certainty there, it was. So she smiled, and the smile that he returned to her seemed to settle in her heart, warming her from the inside out like fine brandy, delicious and every bit as potent. An odd kind of happiness bloomed with that smile, tentative, teetering on a knife's edge, dangerously tempting, and though she knew better Bea grasped it, holding onto it as tightly as she could.

❄ ❄ ❄ ❄ ❄

Justin could not remember the last time he'd set foot in a church. Perhaps the time one of his ne'er–do-well friends had married an opera dancer while out of his head on a mixture of brandy and opium. He wondered what had happened to the happy couple, trying to conjure up the fellow's name and failing. Friends, or what passed for them, had come and gone back then, people passing in and out of his life without his paying much mind to them, or them to him. They were simply partners in crime whilst the fun lasted, and when it—or the money—ran out, they ran out too.

He turned, gazing at his wife's lovely profile as she listened to the sermon. Light from the huge stained-glass window filtered down upon her face, giving her an ethereal, otherworldly beauty that made his breath catch. What benign force had sent her crashing into the terrible darkness of his existence, he could not imagine, could not begin to understand why he would be given such a chance, such a magnificent, extraordinary opportunity, but he was determined to spend the rest of his days proving himself worthy of the gift he'd been given. Beatrice would not leave when the fun ran out, and he would never again do anything to risk the fortune she had put in his hands. He would give her no reason to wish to be anywhere but at his side. He had thought at first that, if his years of flirting and debauchery had taught him anything, it was how to please a woman, but Beatrice was no bored widow looking for distraction, no misbehaving wife wanting to find the excitement her husband could not or would not supply. The rules he had learned so well did not apply to her, and so he had done as she asked and treated her as he might a friend, or a sister, and had been rewarded by discovering a woman he respected and liked so well he could not bear to be out of her company.

The vicar droned on, the words of the sermon passing Justin by, but he closed his eyes, sending his own private prayer to whomever might be listening.

Please, forgive me for being such a fool, for wasting my life on frivolity and pleasure seeking. Please, help me not to mess it up. Please.

❄ ❄ ❄ ❄ ❄

Mrs Kershaw gave Justin a dubious glance as he set foot into her domain. He felt ridiculously as if he were trespassing by entering the kitchens, despite it being his house.

"Justin!"

His wife's exclamation and her accompanying smile chased such feelings away, making him grin like a fool.

"Did you think I would forget?" he asked as she hurried to him, taking his hands.

"No, indeed, but I thought perhaps you might think it too silly," she admitted.

He shook his head, finding he could not look away from her. Beatrice's eyes were more hazel than green in this light, flecked with gold, and he wished Mrs Kershaw and her staff far away so he might lean down and press his mouth against hers. Her lips looked soft, rosy pink, and longing hit him like a fist, striking him square in the chest. "I'm happy with anything that promises good fortune, even though I think I've been so lucky in the past few weeks that I might be accused of greed."

She flushed at his words, turning away from him in confusion. "Well, we are ready to begin. If you would like to wash your hands." She gestured to where a bowl of water awaited him, with a cake of soap and a soft cloth.

Justin did as he was told, watching Beatrice as she helped Mrs Kershaw bring down jars filled with dried fruit. Once he was suitably prepared, Beatrice explained they needed to make up a mixture of dried fruit.

"This is my grandmother's recipe," she said, and instructed him to measure out a quantity of fat sultanas. He watched as Beatrice chopped up dates and figs and sticky prunes, adding the whole to a large pan with a mixture of orange and lemon juice. "And a splash of brandy," she said with a grin.

Justin caught her hand as she added the brandy, tipping the bottle up again when she had finished. "A little drop more," he whispered in her ear.

She tsked at him, shaking her head. "Stop misbehaving or I shan't let you stir," she said, pretending to be cross, though she was obviously trying not to laugh.

He felt ridiculously pleased with himself for the way she teased him. Justin wondered if she knew she was flirting with him and experienced a rush of tenderness when he remembered how innocent she was, how inexperienced. Longing hit him in the same moment, tinged by panic as he knew how easily he could mess things up. But perhaps he would be a better husband for knowing that. If he were young and foolish and knew no better, he might not realise the value of what was before him, might not understand how very precious this fragile thing that bloomed between them truly was. He was a very long way from innocent, had seen the darkest parts of life, of people, and knew he would protect this feeling, would protect *her*, with a ferocity he had felt for nothing in his life before.

He watched Beatrice and Mrs Kershaw, surprised by his own interest as they added softened butter and brown sugar, then put the pan on the range and brought the mixture to the boil.

"Now we mix the dry ingredients," Beatrice said, once the pan had been set aside to cool.

They mixed flour, spices, and ground almonds before adding them to the fruit and stirring in the eggs.

"Now it's your turn," Beatrice said, handing him the spoon.

Justin took it from her, enveloped in the scent of spices rising from the warm, gooey mixture. "That's all?" he asked, raising an eyebrow.

"You can make a wish," she said, her voice soft as she smiled at him.

He nodded and closed his eyes for a moment, stirring the stiff mixture with care, wondering if he would do this again with Beatrice next year, and the year after, and for all the years to come. Justin smiled then, knowing what his wish was.

Opening his eyes, he found her watching him.

"Your turn," he said, relinquishing the spoon.

Beatrice took it, biting her lip as she gazed down at the sticky contents. She closed her eyes and stirred, and when she opened her eyes again and looked up at him, a blush staining her cheeks. What had she wished for, he wondered, knowing that if he were granted another turn, he would ask to have the answer revealed to him.

"And now we must cook it," she said, smiling at him. "And feed it every week until just before Christmas, when we will cover it with marchpane and icing."

"Feed it?" he asked with interest.

"Yes," she replied, mischief dancing in her eyes. "With brandy."

"I cannot wait for Christmas!" Justin exclaimed, making her laugh at him and shake her head. "Is there nothing to eat now? All this hard work has me famished," he said, though the hunger he felt was not for food, but for her, for more of her, sweet and tart and in his arms, willingly, wanting him above all things.

Beatrice nodded, turning to the rather intimidating cook. "Mrs Kershaw, might we have tea and cake in my parlour, please?"

"Of course, my lady. I've a splendid ginger cake which I've been wanting you to try. I made it fresh this morning, and it's my own recipe."

"Oh, that sounds divine," Beatrice said happily, washing her hands and taking off her apron. "Will you join me for tea, then, my lord?" she asked, and he wondered what she would do if she knew how thoroughly besotted he was, what he would do just to have another moment of her time.

"I will."

She glanced up at him uncertainly, hearing something in his voice he had not meant for her to hear. He smiled at her reassuringly, reminding himself that he would behave himself if it killed him, though he suspected it might. Could one die of repressed desire? Having repressed nothing in his life before, he did not know but feared it was all too possible.

Justin followed her to the cosy parlour and imagined spending his evenings with her here every night, imagined knowing that he could soon take her up to bed and make love to her. Images assaulted his hungry mind of his wife in his bed, their bodies entwined, her mouth upon his, her hands on his skin. Justin sucked in an unsteady breath as his body stirred, and he forced his wicked thoughts onto a safer path to get himself under control before he frightened or disgusted her and undid all the progress he'd made.

Though it was barely mid-afternoon, the light was already fading outside, and he watched as Beatrice moved around the room, lighting the lamps. Justin bent and added another log to the fire, watching sparks glitter up the chimney as the eager flames devoured it.

"Shall I draw the curtains?" she asked, peering outside into the gloom. "I think it's raining."

Justin went to stand beside her on the pretext of looking out too, when in truth he wanted to be near her. Though he feared he would overstep the mark, he could not resist the urge to put his hand on her waist as he looked out. "It is," he agreed, looking down at her. "It is cold and wet and wintery, and here we are tucked up in the warm with the promise of tea and cake by the fire. How fortunate we are."

His voice was low, intimate, and he knew he was no longer treating her like a sister, as she had asked of him, but he could not do it, not now, not with everything he felt bursting inside him like fireworks, desperate to be seen.

"Yes," Beatrice said, gazing up at him, the word little more than a breath of sound. He stared down at her, willing her to give him a sign that he did not disgust her, that kissing him wasn't something she could not bear to consider. The flush in her cheeks was encouraging, but then her gaze fell to his lips, settling there, and Justin could not wait a second longer.

He lowered his head, pressing his mouth against hers, keeping his touch light, trying to ensure he did not frighten her away from him, startled and delighted when she gasped against his lips. Her arms rose to coil around his neck, pulling him closer. The invitation was too delicious to refuse, though he feared she did not know how badly he desired her, how hard he had to fight to keep his hands at her waist instead of wandering and exploring as they longed to do.

She pulled away from him and though he was desperate for more, mad with the need to plunder and devour and taste every sweet inch of her skin, he let her go.

"The tea will be here any moment," she said a little unsteadily, avoiding his gaze.

"Beatrice," he said, reaching for her hand, praying he had not ruined things.

She allowed him to take hold of her fingers for a moment before offering him a shy smile. "I prefer Bea, if you don't mind."

"Bea," he repeated, letting out a breath. "Anything you want, love."

There was a quiet knock before a footman entered, carrying in the tea tray.

Bea thanked him and the footman left them alone once more. "Oh, this smells divine," she said, cutting a slice of the ginger cake Mrs Kershaw had promised.

She put it on a plate and then broke a large piece off, popping it in her mouth and chewing with a soft sigh of pleasure that hit Justin like a glittering shaft of bright desire, piercing his good intentions. He sat down before he could do something unforgiveable and haul her into his arms, taking her mouth with all the passion he felt for her.

"May I try?" the words were out before he could stop them, old instincts kicking in when he knew, *knew* he was treading on thin ice.

She smiled at him and walked over, offering him what remained of the slice so he could break a piece off as she had done. Justin shook his head wordlessly, and she stilled, her gaze once more falling to his mouth. He waited, his heart thudding with anticipation as she hesitated. He watched, noticing the slight tremble of her fingers as she broke a piece off and offered it up to him, the look in her eyes that of a woman holding out a treat to something wild and dangerous that might devour her instead of the morsel she held. She wasn't wrong.

He opened his mouth, an obedient creature hiding his fangs, pretending domesticity. No, not pretending, he amended silently: *trying*. Trying harder than he'd tried for anything in his life, but he was not an angel, not beyond tempting her a little, hoping desperately he *was* a temptation to her.

She popped the piece of cake into his mouth, her breath hitching as her fingers touched his lips. Before he could counsel himself into restraint, remind himself to go carefully, Justin reached for her, his hands settling on her hips. She gasped, surprised, but did not scurry away. Instead, she stared down at him, breathing hard as he pulled a little, allowing her the opportunity to run if she wished to. She didn't run, and Justin pulled her harder, tumbling her down into his lap.

She gave a little squeak of surprise, almost drowned out by the delicious rustle of petticoats and skirts.

"I have wanted to do that since the first night I saw you. I do not know how I have restrained myself for this long," he admitted, hearing his own words as something dark and decadent. He wished it were not so, but perhaps that wicked voice would always be a part of him, only now he would keep it for her alone, to delight his wife and bring her all the pleasures he had learnt during his fall from grace.

She swallowed, gazing up at him, her lovely eyes wide and guileless. "I think I have wanted you to do it for that long too," she whispered, the admission striking deep in his heart, making his breath catch. "You looked like a beautiful monster, a fallen angel, and I knew I would need to keep you at a distance, or I should be caught in your toils, and here I am," she added with a breathless laugh.

Justin paused, hearing the fear there and disliking it.

He reached out a hand, stroking her satiny cheek. "Foolish girl," he whispered, shaking his head. "Have you still not realised that I am the one caught, held fast, your willing captive for as long as you wish to keep me beside you?"

She blinked up at him, breathing hard, tension thrumming through her.

"Always, Justin," she said, making his heart soar.

He pulled her close, pressing his mouth to hers, kissing her harder than he had intended, forgetting his promise to go slowly, not to frighten her, but Bea was not afraid. Bea had never been afraid of him; she was braver and bolder than anyone he had ever known. Braver than he had ever been, and now she was putting her heart in his hands though she knew it was a risk or believed it to be so. Silently, he promised her he would never do her harm, gentling his kisses, softening the crushing embrace of his arms, teaching her the give and take and intimacy of kisses in a way he was uncertain he had ever learned himself. Not like this, not how it felt with her, as a melding of souls, not just mouths.

Justin held her there, kissing and kissing and content to do nothing more, though his body strained with desire. For her, he could wait, though it was a delicious torment to have her so near and not take everything he wanted. Yet he would wait willingly, giving of himself and his time as he had never been willing to do before.

The tea went cold, the fire dying by slow degrees until Justin heard the bell sound, announcing dinner would be ready in fifteen minutes.

Bea gasped, looking delightfully rumpled, her mouth swollen from his kisses, her hair all coming undone. "Dinner!" she exclaimed, staring at him as though he had cast some spell over her. "We've been here for… for hours."

She blushed a glorious shade of pink that only made Justin want to fluster her still more thoroughly. Before he could do so, she wriggled out of his lap, doing terrible things to his equilibrium as her plump bottom squirmed against his groin.

"So we have," he said, smiling lazily at her.

She glared at him and then made a spluttering sound, somewhere between a giggle and snort, covering her mouth with her hand.

"Oh," she said crossly, though she did not look cross in the least. "You… You… devil!" With that, she shook her head, biting her lip and sending him one last look of amused exasperation. "We shall dine together tonight, don't be late," she called to him, before she hurried out and closed the door behind her.

Chapter 11

"Wherein the perfect day becomes fodder for the gossip mill."

27th November 1820.

"Come along, slugabed. If you're still planning on shopping in Tunbridge Wells, you need to get a move on."

Rachel's voice pierced Bea's sleepy brain, and she burrowed deeper into the warm blankets. A cold bright light filled the room as Rachel drew the curtains, promising another freezing morning, and chasing away the remnants of a delicious dream where Bea was held securely on Justin's lap, his strong arms around her, his lips tender upon hers, kissing her endlessly. She blinked her eyes open, fingers reaching to touch her mouth in astonishment as reality returned with a rush of remembered images and sensations.

"Oh," she said, a soft exclamation that Rachel did not hear, thank heavens. Blushing, Bea hid under the covers for a moment, pretending reluctance to get up while she composed herself. They had kissed for… for hours, she realised, a startled laugh bubbling in her throat, and then… and then she had gone down to dinner, half afraid, wondering if he would assume that, having given him such encouragement, she would take him to her bed.

But Justin had not assumed, he had not taken advantage. Instead, he had been careful with her, solicitous, gently flirtatious but cautious not to do or say anything that made her feel uncomfortable. Yet she had seen the banked fire in his eyes, had felt the smouldering heat of everything that lay between them, still unsaid, untried. If she spoke words of encouragement, or gave him a sign, he would devour her in that heat.

It had been Justin who had suggested the shopping trip today, he who had offered to escort her to Tunbridge Wells to visit the shops, and to take the water if she desired. Knowing that she would see him again when she went down to breakfast, and on the journey into town—and that they would sit side-by-side in the carriage for a journey of close to two hours—made her heart skip with anticipation. She wanted to see him, desperately wanted another evening of kisses in his arms, and yet she was still afraid, afraid of what she felt for him, this man who had tasted so many women, had drunk so deep of every wicked pleasure he'd ruined himself. *Almost,* she amended. He had *almost* ruined himself, but he had drawn back now, because of her.

Her happiness dimmed as she wondered if she could be enough to keep him from returning to that world, if she would be enough to make him turn away from temptation day after day, for years to come. Perhaps she was merely a novelty, something he would grow tired of. *No.* Justin had explained what had driven him onto the path he'd taken: the deaths of his parents, the terrible misunderstanding of what his father had hoped for him. He was happy with her, happier than he had ever been before. He had said so. It was hard to believe, though, when she had never captured any man's attention before, certainly not a man like Justin, so handsome and sophisticated in all the ways Bea was not. Her father had been in no hurry to marry her off, to deprive himself of her company, and so although she'd had her come out, it had not been with any serious intention of finding a husband. She had never spent much time flirting, considering this man or that as a potential mate and, after last night, she did not know how to be with Justin.

So, it was with such unsettling thoughts in her heart that Bea made her way to the breakfast room with trepidation. Justin was there and set aside his paper when he saw her, smiling warmly as he got to his feet.

"Good morning, love. Did you sleep well?"

Bea nodded, avoiding his gaze as she moved to take her place, but Justin stopped her, moving closer and taking her hand, lifting it to his lips.

"Bea," he said softly. "Don't be afraid of me. I am all at sea too, you know. I've never… never done *this* before, either," he told her with a helpless laugh.

She smiled up at him, disarmed as always by his candour, by his blue eyes full of gentle amusement. She let out a breath. "I'm sorry, I… I didn't know how to face you after—"

He kissed her, a swift brush of his lips against hers. "There," he said. "The worst is over. Now you need not spend the morning sat upon thorns, worrying if I will kiss you, for it has already happened."

She laughed, startled and delighted at once. "But will you do it again?" she demanded, finding it easy again to tease and talk with him.

"Bea, love, you cannot expect me to give away all my secrets," he scolded, sounding so grave she shook her head, accepting his help as he pulled out her chair for her.

"I suppose not," she said ruefully, accepting a cup of tea from a footman who appeared silently at her elbow, and asking for a bowl of porridge. She wondered if the man had seen her husband kissing her and decided she did not care if he had.

They broke their fast, chatting comfortably about the things they wished to do in Tunbridge Wells. Bea explained her need for ink, and a desire to buy Christmas gifts. She did not have many people to buy for any longer, but she thought she would send a token to Dorothy, and she wished to get Rachel something special, and… and then there was Justin.

❄ ❄ ❄ ❄ ❄

Justin watched the countryside as it passed by, feeling a surge of pleasure at the sight of the beautiful scenery, at once so familiar and yet somehow new and different. He smiled as he realised it was not the scenery that was different but himself. Usually such journeys were accompanied by a terrible hangover, the familiar landscape viewed with the sickening realisation that he was coming home because he had shamed himself again, dishonoured his already blackened name a shade darker. He considered that, wondering if he might forgive himself for some of that bad behaviour, perhaps even pity himself for all he had missed out on because of the choices he'd made. But he had never murdered anyone, never fought anyone who did not deserve a beating, never bedded a woman who hadn't wished it, and if he'd cheated at cards a time or two, it had been because he'd been desperate. There were those who might despise him for his past, but if Bea didn't, perhaps he need not do so either. The thought was heartening and made him view the future with hope, with the expectation that *he could* do better.

Today, he was taking an outing with his wife to choose Christmas presents, to give her a pleasant day out because he wished to please her. It was such an innocuous pleasure, such a simple thing to do, that he wondered at the delight he took in it, something that most other people took for granted. Outside, the fields and trees seemed frozen in place, rimed with hoarfrost, thick and velvety white, the world dressed in a seasonal mantle as though he had ordered such perfection and been granted his every wish. He turned to Bea, moving to tuck the blanket more securely around her. They had stopped half an hour ago to replace the heated brick for her feet, but it must be cooling by now.

"You are warm enough?" he asked. "I do not wish you to arrive as a little ice block."

She laughed and shook her head. "I am perfectly cosy, thank you. It was a splendid idea, and I am looking forward to shopping. It's been a long time since I could visit the shops. I must warn you, however, that if you allow me inside a bookshop, I may become unreasonable if you try to make me leave."

"Ah, I see. I've been duped into marrying a bluestocking. Bea, how could you?" he said reproachfully.

She snorted, which delighted him for reasons he did not understand. "You may say such things in jest, my lord, but get between me and a novel I have not yet read, and you may find those words come back to haunt you."

He grinned and gave a shrug. "Ah, well, now you have given me something to aim for. I never could resist temptation, remember?" Her face fell and Justin kicked himself. *Fool!* What a stupid thing to say. "Bea." His voice was low, urgent, as he reached for her hand. "I did not mean that. I was only—"

"I know," she said, her smile returning as she glanced up at him. "It's only I—"

"I know," he said, his voice firm, not wanting her to have to say the words, to make herself more vulnerable than he knew she was already. "But there is nothing, nothing for you to worry about. I—"

He cast around for the right words, wanting to tell her he needed her and her alone, that every mistake he had ever made had prepared him for this, to be ready for this, to appreciate what he'd been given. The fates had forged him in dark fires, had drowned him over and again in vice, so he might break free and know without doubt that there was no temptation worth giving into, no patch of grass that could ever be greener, no pleasure greater than those he might find with his own wife.

But Bea's lips found his, pressing softly, shyly against his mouth, chasing away thought and filling his heart with joy. She pulled back, smiling at him.

"I know, Justin. You got lost, I think, and there was no one to show you there was another path, but perhaps we could find the way together now, If... if you wish to."

Justin stared at her in wonder. If he *wished* to?

"Bea, I—" he began, not knowing what to say but Bea was not done yet.

"I love you."

Justin's breath caught. The words were so unexpected he could hardly comprehend that they had been given so easily, willingly, and not until they were uttered did he realise how desperately he had wanted to hear them.

"Bea," he said, defenceless against the emotions rising inside him, wanting to tell her everything he felt and finding the words would not come he was so overwhelmed. So, instead he kissed her, hoping she felt in his touch, in his kiss, all that he could not speak aloud, not yet. He kissed her and held nothing back of himself, hid no corner of his heart, kissing her as though he were drowning and she were air, as though she was the salvation he had been searching for his entire life… and he knew it was nothing but the truth.

❄ ❄ ❄ ❄ ❄

Bea stepped down from the carriage on legs that did not feel entirely steady. Her heart was light, her mind giddy with happiness, with the enormity of the risk she had taken. She did not regret it, she assured herself. How could she, when she had seen the look in Justin's eyes, the happiness and depth of feeling she had sensed in him? His kiss had been everything and more than she had ever believed a kiss could be after too many hours reading romance novels and dreaming of handsome heroes of the kind she knew could not exist.

He took her arm, his gaze upon hers warm and reassuring as they walked towards the famous Pantiles and the elegant shops and tearooms to be found there.

"Should you like to take tea first, before we begin?" Justin asked and then laughed as he realised a bookshop had already taken her attention. "Ah, I see. Well, I suppose you did warn me."

"I did," she replied with a rueful smile. "Do you mind? If you are bored, you could meet me back here and—"

"If you think I am letting you out of my sight in such a place, you are much mistaken," he said, shaking his head. "Heaven alone knows what might happen. You might buy the entire shop and refuse to ever leave it."

"I might," she admitted with a laugh.

"No, no. Besides, what makes you think I am immune to the lure of a good story? I do read things other than the sporting journals, you know."

"You do?" she asked, genuinely interested.

"I do," he said firmly. "Just because I was forced to sell every book I owned, does not mean I do not value them and wish to restock the library at Chalfont. Come, perhaps I shall buy every book for you after all," he said with a wink, guiding her inside.

They spent a happy hour in the bookshop and Bea found herself charmed when Justin insisted on buying her the books she had chosen, adding a recipe book at the last moment to give to Mrs Kershaw.

"She scares me," he told her confidentially, pulling a face. "I'm trying to bribe my way into her good books."

"Foolish creature," Bea said, laughing at his antics. "But I don't doubt it will work, and it has the bonus of giving us lovely things to eat. Well done."

"Not just a pretty face, love," he whispered in her ear, his warm breath making her shiver as she waited for the shop owner to wrap their purchases. Justin carried them for her, and they moved onto the next shop, finding the ink she had wanted and buying some writing paper, too. They stopped for a while at a pretty tea shop to warm up, sitting in the window and watching the fashionable people parade up and down. Bea ordered a cup of hot chocolate, and they shared a plate of shortbread, chatting contentedly as Bea wracked her brain for something that Justin might like for Christmas.

Once thawed out, they returned to their shopping, with Bea finding a lovely yellow silk scarf for Rachel that Bea knew she would adore, and a pair of kid gloves that exactly matched the pretty shade. They were perusing a jeweller's shop window, when Bea's gaze lit upon a delicate gold cravat pin, with a large sapphire at the head. The colour was the same dark blue as Justin's eyes, and her heart skipped as she realised she had found the perfect gift.

Not wishing to give herself away, she allowed them to stroll on, going into several more shops before she stopped him outside.

"Justin, there is something I wish to buy, but I do not wish you to come with me," she said, smiling at him.

He frowned at her for a moment before his expression cleared, his smile so boyishly pleased her heart felt squeezed in her chest. "You're buying me a Christmas present!" he exclaimed.

Bea rolled her eyes. "Well, I might, if you go away for a moment." She made a little shooing motion, but he hesitated.

"I don't like to leave you alone," he said, a little anxiously.

"It's only for a moment," she protested, laughing at his concern. "Fifteen minutes is all I need. I shall meet you back here, in this very spot."

Justin sighed and then nodded. "Very well, love. Give me those parcels and I will drop them back with our coachman. There's a tobacconist next to the inn where he's waiting, and I can buy John some cigars for Christmas. It might stop him from stealing mine," he added with a grin.

Bea nodded and then gasped as he leaned in and kissed her.

"Justin!" she said in shock, looking around to see if anyone had noticed.

He returned an unrepentant grin before he turned and strode away. Bea watched him go, admiring his elegant figure, the broad shoulders and the gold hair that shone beneath his hat.

Sighing and telling herself she was in a bad way, she hurried back to the jewellers.

❆ ❆ ❆ ❆ ❆

Justin whistled softly to himself as he walked back to meet Bea. It hadn't yet been fifteen minutes, but he was too eager to be in her company again to dally. He tried to remember a time in his life when he had ever been this happy and could bring nothing to mind. Even those weeks with his father had been overshadowed by knowing the man had never been interested in him before then, and the anxiety that he would not be so again. What had come next had forever tainted those memories, but somehow Bea had even given him back those, allowing him to think of his father with affection and pity instead of a spoiled mixture of childish hero worship and resentment.

Lost in thought, Justin turned back into The Pantiles as a woman ran forward, clutching at his arm.

"Rutherford? Oh! It is you," she cried in relief. "Thank heavens. I wrote to you this very morning, but my prayers have been answered."

Justin gazed in horror, a cold sensation of dread washing over him as he stared into the beautiful face of Mrs Lavinia Jenkins. He shook off her hand, glaring at her.

"I cannot think what more you can possibly ask of me," Justin replied, anger rising as he looked around to see if Bea was watching.

To his relief, she was not yet waiting for him, but other people had seen and knew what a scandalous couple they were regarding. Gossip would run riot. Justin had recognised a few people that morning and hoped that Bea had not noticed them cut him. To his surprise, he hadn't much cared for his own sake, but he wanted nothing to upset his wife or cut up her peace.

"Oh, Rutherford, I know I have no right to ask, but I am desperate," she said, resting her hand on her swollen belly.

Justin cursed, knowing he could not in all conscience leave her to her fate with a child on the way. "What has happened?" he demanded. "I thought you said you had money enough, that your aunt had left you to live comfortably."

Lavinia snorted at that. "Comfortably," she exclaimed in disgust. "Hardly that, but I get by. That's not the problem," she said urgently.

"Then what is? Tell me quickly before my wife sees you."

"It's my husband," she said, reaching out and taking his arm. "Rutherford, I'm frightened."

Justin regarded her with concern, realising he was not seeing playacting, she really was afraid. Where her husband was concerned, she likely had good reason. Not that they were actually married now. Justin had been named in the dreadful crimcon. The scandal of his public revelation of their affair had been bad enough, the following duel worse still, but the trial had finally ruined him and sent him to ground. Mr Jenkins was a respected politician and one that other men of the ton could empathise with. Justin had been cast as nothing but a pleasure-seeking rake who'd ruined a man's innocent wife before she'd given him the requisite heir and a spare. That was about as dishonourable as it got.

A sharp-edged giggle caught his attention, and he looked up, his heart sinking to his boots as he saw Beatrice had emerged from whatever shop she'd been inside, buying him a Christmas gift. Everyone was watching her avidly, and she was staring at him… and at Lavinia. All the colour drained from her lovely face, her expression one of such shock he feared she might faint.

No, he begged whatever deity might listen to a man like him. *Please, no.*

❄ ❄ ❄ ❄ ❄

Beatrice hurried from the jeweller's shop, feeling very pleased with herself. In her mind she could see Justin wearing the elegant sapphire in his snowy white cravat, knew the way it would highlight the stunning blue of his eyes. She hoped he would like it as much as she did.

There seemed quite a crowd gathered in the place where she was to meet Justin, and Bea wondered at it, wondered why they turned to look upon her with such expressions of delight. She smiled back, tentatively, uncertain whether those looks were entirely friendly, and then their gazes moved as one, towards an intimate little scene at the entrance to The Pantiles.

Justin was there, his head bent, his expression one of concern as a beautiful woman reached and put her hand on his arm. The gesture seemed an intimate one, and Bea's gaze fell to the woman's obvious pregnancy, her full belly pronouncing the fact she was at least six months gone.

"It's his mistress, Lavinia Jenkins," she heard someone say, their voice too loud, loud enough to ensure she heard it. "She's carrying his child, of course. That's why her husband divorced her. Such a scandal! And Rutherford admitted it to the man's face, can you imagine?"

Bea stood very still. The ground seemed to shift under her feet, tilting her world onto its side. *Fool!* yelled a voice in her head. *Fool, fool, fool! He's caught you in his web just like he does every woman. It's all lies, it's all —*

Bea silenced the voice, ignoring the smattering of giggles and snide remarks that reached her ears as Justin looked up, his expression horrified as he saw her watching. Bea saw too, the way his shoulders sagged, the look of defeat that shadowed his eyes, believing she would walk away from him.

For a moment, Bea considered doing just that, except… except she had known about Mrs Jenkins. No, she had not known she was carrying Justin's child, but… but that had been before she knew him. He had changed since then. *She* had changed him. He had told her so, and she had believed it. She had fallen in love with him knowing he'd been appalling, knowing he'd been wicked and awful and had brought shame upon himself, and she had still found a man worth loving. The least she could do was give him a chance to explain, and if Mrs Jenkins was carrying his child, it was only right that he made provision for it. No wonder the woman looked so frantic.

So Bea put up her chin, giving the gossiping crowd around her a sweeping look of disdain, before walking towards her husband.

"Justin," she said, astonished to hear her voice sounded perfectly calm when she was shaking inside. "Would you introduce me to your friend?"

Mrs Jenkins stared at her in obvious astonishment, though her expression was nothing compared to Justin's, who gazed at her open-mouthed.

"Bea," he said helplessly. "Bea, I didn't, we haven't—"

Reaching out, Bea took his arm and patted it gently. "It's all right, my lord. You will have the chance to explain everything to me, but I believe this lady—Mrs Jenkins, is it? —seems to be in some distress. Perhaps we could go somewhere more private to speak with her."

Mrs Jenkins seemed to rally at that. "You are all kindness, Lady Rutherford," she said, curtseying and having the grace to blush at the situation. "I live just a few steps around the corner, if you would be so good as to come with me."

"Certainly," Bea said, nodding. "Come, Justin."

Justin seemed to shake himself out of whatever trance he was in and nodded, guiding her in Mrs Jenkins's wake and leaving the excited crowd to make what they would of the extraordinary scene.

"Bea," Justin said urgently as they walked. "You must let me explain to you."

Bea looked up, seeing the fear in his eyes. That steadied her, knowing that he was afraid of losing her good opinion. "I will," she told him, offering him a tentative smile.

Perhaps she was being an unutterable fool, but women were foolish in love, were they not? Why should she be any different?

Chapter 12

"Wherein the truth is revealed, for better or for worse."

27th November 1820.

She had smiled at him. Justin clung to that, hoping against hope that she would allow him to explain everything, that this collision with his dreadful past would not ruin it all. Numbly, he escorted her after Mrs Jenkins, wondering what on earth the wretched woman would have from him now. He knew he ought not to be angry with her; it was her husband who had created this damnable situation, but having been so close to happiness to now risk losing it all was something he could not face with equanimity.

Mrs Jenkins's home was a small, terraced property, facing directly onto the street. It was far smaller and shabbier than everything she had left behind, and Justin knew he should not judge her too harshly. She had done what she had for the right reasons as, for once, had he.

She showed them into a small, dark parlour where a lacklustre fire burned. Mrs Jenkins lit a lamp, which improved the ambiance somewhat, and a maid hurried in, from whom the lady ordered tea. Still, it was about as awkward a situation as any he'd faced during his less than illustrious career as a libertine, and that was saying something.

"Well," Bea said, taking off her bonnet and laying it to one side before facing Mrs Jenkins. "I assume you are petitioning my husband for the sake of your child. Please, let me assure you, that if there is responsibility, Justin will do the right thing by you. Won't you, Justin?" she said, and there was that smile again, tentative but full of understanding.

She would forgive him, he realised then, his heart expanding so he did not know if his chest could contain the feeling. His wife believed this woman's child was his, and she would not hate him for it.

"It's not mine!" The words exploded from him before he could think of a more elegant way of putting it, but he didn't much care, so long as she knew. "Lavinia was never my lover. It was all a sham."

Bea stared at him, wide-eyed, and then gave a choked laugh. "Oh," she said, a harsh breath leaving her as tears sparkled in her eyes. "Oh, that's… that's good."

She sat down heavily, as if whatever force of will had kept her upright had left her in a rush.

"Bea," he cried, sitting down beside her and taking her hands, raising first one and then the other to his lips. "Bea, I shall never disgrace you so, I swear it. I know I might give you cause for embarrassment in the future, when my past rears its ugly head and shames us both, but I swear upon all that I hold dear, that I will never betray you. Please, love, please bel—"

"I believe you." The words were quiet but spoken with certainty, her calm green gaze settling upon him like a benediction.

"You… You do?" She nodded, and Justin let out a breath. "Thank God for you, Bea. Thank God."

He looked up then to see Lavinia watching them anxiously. A nervous smile curved her lips. "Well, Rutherford, I never thought to see you of all men brought to your knees by love. Certainly not by your wife! How the ladies of the *ton* will weep to discover your icy heart has finally been thawed. They called him the Winter Rogue, you know," she added, speaking now to Bea. "On account of his caring for no one. Not even himself, I think."

"That's enough," Justin said, uncomfortable with the line of conversation. His wife had experienced enough upset for one day without Lavinia making off-colour jokes or references to his reprehensible past. "Tell me what it is that has you in such a taking and do it quickly."

Lavinia flushed but nodded, sitting down beside the fire with little grace, for her burgeoning body made the movement awkward. "I beg you will forgive me my plain speaking, Lady Rutherford, but the truth is, my dolt of a husband has finally realised that I could not have had an affair with your husband. His staff watched me so closely, spying on my every move and reporting back to him that there was no possible way I could have slipped away, even for an hour, without someone noticing. I think he was so incensed by your declaring the affair to his face, Rutherford, that he did not stop to think why I might wish for such a thing."

"You wished to escape?" Bea asked, her expression one of concern.

Justin took her hand and clasped it, wondering at the compassion he saw in his wife's eyes for a woman who was notorious for having an affair with her husband.

Lavinia nodded. "My husband is a brute, my lady. I will tell you now that I was never unfaithful to him, not with Rutherford nor anyone else. But Robert beat me, often, and with enough brutality that, when I fell pregnant, I feared for my child. Fool that I was, I hoped that the promise of an heir would stay his hand. I was wrong."

"Oh, Mrs Jenkins. I cannot imagine how frightened you must have been," Bea said, such genuine regret in her voice that Lavinia's eyes filled with tears.

"I hope you cannot. I know you never will with Rutherford at least. I envy you that much. I was in love once, you know, and my sweetheart offered for me, but my father forbade the match and forced me to marry Robert. A far more suitable match in his opinion."

"Oh, how I detest the meddling of men!" Bea said furiously. "Why is it a woman cannot decide for herself who is to have the keeping of her. At least any mistakes would be our own. I am so sorry, Mrs Jenkins, for all you have endured, and that you have been treated so ill," Bea said, her obvious rage making the woman smile.

"Why, how passionate you are, my lady, and compassionate too. Now, I see why you love her so, Rutherford."

"For that and for a good many other reasons," Justin said softly, smiling as Bea blushed scarlet.

Lavinia carried on her story, speaking directly to Bea. "I was frightened and desperate, knowing there was no one who would help me. I tried to contact my old sweetheart, hoping he might help me, but he returned to France after my marriage, and if he did contact me, I fear Robert destroyed his letters. I tried telling my friends that Robert beat me, but they only became embarrassed and said such things were between a man and his wife. Then, during a party, Justin stepped in when Robert…Well, he was angry with me for something, I don't even remember what, but Robert took me outside onto the terrace and would have slapped me for my misdemeanour there and then, only Justin was there, and he caught Robert's hand. He told him only the lowest kind of man laid hands on a woman, and that he prayed Robert was not quite that contemptible."

Justin experienced the oddest sensation as Bea turned her gaze upon him, pride shining in her eyes. Pride? For *him?* The sensation flooded him, warm and soothing, smoothing off rough edges and tending wounds that had festered for decades. She was proud of him, and anything now seemed possible.

"That sounds like my husband," she said, turning back to Lavinia.

Lavinia nodded. "I admit, I did not realise then what an honourable man Rutherford was. When I asked what I did of him, I did not understand what I would do to him. I believed his name already so black another such scandal would not touch him or cause him a moment's distress. I was wrong, and… and I am sorry, Rutherford, sorry for all that befell you because you were kind to me. I am most sincerely sorry that you were so grievously hurt in that duel. Please know that I prayed for you daily, prayed that you would recover and find happiness."

Justin nodded, finding that her words helped somewhat, knowing that she recognised he had sacrificed a good deal for a woman he barely knew. Perhaps he *had* done something to earn his wife's arrival in his life.

"When Rutherford told Robert we were having an affair, in public, it forced his hand. He had to divorce me or become a laughingstock. Rutherford took me in for a few days until I could arrange a place of my own. I lived close to London while the dreadful crimcon continued, but then I moved away, hoping to be a little less notorious, and I have been here ever since." She gestured to the cramped little parlour with a wan smile. "Do not pity me too much, my lady. My reduced circumstances are trying, but I would not swap this for a beautiful house and pretty gowns and a man who hurt me without caring most every day."

"Believe me, I understand," Bea said, and Justin squeezed her fingers, knowing she was remembering the circumstances under which she had sought him out.

"So now Robert has realised the child is his, he's threatening to take it from you once it is born?" Justin guessed.

Lavinia nodded, her face crumpling. "Yes," she said, dabbing her eyes with a handkerchief. But I have a plan, Rutherford, and… and I only need a little help. I know I have no right to ask after you did so much for me already."

"Name it," Bea said, her voice firm. "No man who would beat his wife should have the right to do so to a child. Tell us what you need, and we shall see to it. Won't we, Justin?"

She looked up at him, such trust in her eyes that Justin knew he was hopelessly, irrevocably in love with his wife. "Yes, love," he said, nodding at her. "We'll do anything we can to help."

❄ ❄ ❄ ❄ ❄

Bea leaned against Justin as the carriage took them home to Chalfont. She felt exhausted, as if she had overcome some terrible trial. She had, she supposed, remembering when she had seen Justin with Mrs Jenkins. For a moment her happiness had teetered on a knife's edge, everything she had dreamed of and hoped for, weighed in the balance.

How glad she was she had not assumed the worst, that she had given him the chance to explain things. She might have ruined everything by throwing accusations around, for even though Justin could have proven his innocence, she would have hurt him by not trusting him, would have damaged the belief he'd begun to have in himself, that he could have the life he had turned his back on as a grieving boy.

"Thank you."

His voice was quiet and solemn as the carriage rumbled through the lanes, twilight casting shadows along the lanes as they drew close to home. They had barely spoken since leaving Mrs Jenkins, but it had not been an uneasy silence, just a fatigued one. They had both been upset, afraid, their worlds thrown into doubt, and even the relief of realising that it wasn't true seemed to sap their energy. Justin's arms tightened around her as his words settled in her heart.

Bea said nothing. Responding with 'you're welcome' seemed trite somehow, and she did not know how else to reply, so she simply covered his hands with her own.

When they arrived back at Chalfont, Bea asked Rachel to prepare a bath before turning to Justin. He dismissed the footmen and Morley, leaving them alone in the hallway.

"I'll eat in my room tonight," she told him, smiling to soften the blow and to show it wasn't a punishment. "Today has been rather… tiring."

Justin nodded, his expression full of regret as he reached for her hands.

"Bea—"

"No, wait. Nothing has changed," she assured him. "Nothing at all. I meant what I said to you, and I do not regret it."

He closed his eyes and then opened them again, smiling at her. "I will never give you cause to regret it," he told her, his expression grave.

Bea nodded and lifted on her toes to kiss his cheek, wanting to be sure he knew she meant what she said. A prickle of golden stubble pressed against her lips and the strangest sensation uncoiled deep in her belly, liquid and warm. It made her want to press closer, to lower her lips to the place beneath his ear where his pulse thrummed. His scent, starched linen and bergamot and warm male skin, invaded her senses, making her giddy and strangely restless. Unsettled, Bea pushed away from him, offering him a shy smile before she fled, hurrying up the stairs to her room.

❄ ❄ ❄ ❄ ❄

Justin watched his wife run up the stairs, his heart thudding. His skin seemed too tight, as if it no longer fit him. Longing surged through his blood, together with the desire to give chase, to show her all the things she did not understand awaited them both, if only she would let go of the last vestiges of reserve and trust him… but he could not ask for that. Certainly not after the day she'd had. He had hoped to give her a pleasant outing, the first of many, an indication of the life they could share together. Justin smiled as he supposed he had done so, in a way. The first half of their day had been perfection and the rest… well, she had told him she was proud of him, she had told him she did not regret saying she loved him, that nothing had changed.

That was more than he could have believed possible such a short while ago, so he would not be so greedy as to lament another night in a lonely bed, dreaming of the woman he desired above all others. Anticipation was not such a curse after all; it would only make their coming together all the sweeter.

Chapter 13

"Wherein surprises abound."

28th November 1820.

The next morning, Justin awaited his wife in the breakfast parlour, fidgeting impatiently for the sound of her light footsteps. He'd just had news that the present he had bought her had arrived earlier than expected, and he was all eagerness to show it to her.

"Good morning, Justin."

"Bea."

Justin's breath caught as his wife came into the room. She looked stunning in a gown of deep forest green that highlighted the green in her eyes. It fitted beautifully, showing off the curves of her bust and her slender form, making him long to go to her and pull her into his arms. He might have done so too, if a footman had not entered in her wake, pulling out her chair and serving her tea.

Regretting their audience, Justin sat and then waved the servants away impatiently the moment she had been served her breakfast.

"That's a lovely gown, Bea. It suits you."

"Thank you," she replied, smoothing a hand over the fine velvet in a way that made his mouth suddenly dry, imagining his own hand following the same path. "It's new and only arrived yesterday. I ordered some new gowns from the modiste I always used before Papa died. Happily, she has made for me since I was little more than a girl, and knows my measurements by heart, I should think."

"I should say she does," Justin replied, unable to keep the rather lustful note from his words.

She glanced at him uncertainly and he returned a rueful smile. To his relief, Bea laughed and shook her head.

"Did you order a riding habit yet?" he asked, watching her elegant fingers as she buttered a warm roll and added a small spoonful of jam. She nodded, biting into the roll with relish. Justin watched her mouth as she chewed, telling himself not to be so ridiculous. The sight of his wife's mouth ought not to be enough to have his body reacting so forcefully. Yet it was, and he had to take a deep breath to steady himself.

"I did. Not that I've had time to wear it, even if I'd had time to find a horse. I really must, for I miss riding out."

Justin hid a smile and nodded. "Indeed, it is a pity, for I should enjoy riding out with you. There are some lovely paths around Chalfont that I would love to show you. It's such a beautiful morning, too, though cold, I think."

"That does not signify," she said, shaking her head. "I love riding on a cold, crisp morning. There is nothing better, and now you have made me wistful, longing for something I cannot have."

"Have I?" he asked her softly, wondering if she knew how he hungered for her, for the kind of intimacy he longed to share with her.

She held his gaze for a moment, hearing more in his tone than just the words. Bea looked away, and he knew he had unnerved her, but she glanced back at him a moment later, a speculative gleam in her eyes that gave him hope. He winked at her, and she bit her lip, hiding a smile. Justin's heart soared.

When they had finished eating, Justin followed her out of the breakfast parlour. "My Lady Rutherford, might I beg a moment of your time?"

She turned, smiling quizzically at him and his sudden formality. "You may, my lord."

"Excellent! Morley, bring my coat and my lady's cloak and bonnet, there's a good fellow."

Morley nodded, hurrying off.

"Justin, whatever are you up to?" Bea asked, laughing as he strode impatiently up and down until Morley reappeared.

Justin said nothing, only flashed her a grin and bundled her into her cloak, barely giving her time to tie the ribbons of her bonnet before he took her hand, dragging her out of doors.

"Have you gone mad?" she asked, still laughing as he broke into a run, tugging her behind him. She squealed and clutched at her bonnet as she scurried to keep up.

"Mad for you, my love," he called back, wondering if she knew how true the words were as they arrived at the stables. Bea was pink-cheeked and breathless and had never looked lovelier as far as he was concerned.

"Now, stay there, and close your eyes," he told her.

She opened her mouth to protest, but whatever she saw in his expression stilled her tongue and she smiled instead, closing her eyes. Unable to resist the temptation, Justin pressed his mouth to hers, the exquisite pleasure of being able to do such a thing singing through his blood like the finest of champagne.

"Don't move," he whispered against her lips, before hurrying away. "Where is she?" he asked the head groom quietly.

The man saw Bea standing with her eyes closed and grinned. "In here, my lord, and the sweetest creature she is, too, though a tad skittish. My lady will love her, I reckon."

Justin patted the fellow on the shoulder, delighted, and followed him into the newly refurbished stables. He had known the mare was perfect for Bea the moment he had seen her. A dappled grey Arabian, with her finely chiselled head and arching neck, she was the prettiest horse he had ever seen.

He led the mare out, keeping his eyes upon Bea as she stood patiently, awaiting his word.

"You can open your eyes now," he told her, unable to keep a stupid grin from his face.

Bea's eyes opened and settled upon the mare. Justin watched, feeling ridiculously nervous, as her mouth fell open. "Oh! How beautiful. What a splendid horse, Justin, you…" She hesitated, staring at him. "You bought her for me?"

Justin laughed at her incredulity. "Of course I bought her for you, you ridiculous girl. Why else am I standing here?"

"Oh, Justin!" She ran to him, hugging him tightly and kissing his cheek, making him feel about ten feet tall before she turned to the mare and stroked her soft nose.

"She's called Dove," he told her as the mare snuffled at her fingers and the two got to know each other. "And she's got the loveliest manners, but she's got spirit too, just enough to give you a challenge without being overly headstrong."

"I don't know what to say," she said, sounding a little choked. "I never received anything so lovely in all my days. She's beautiful, Justin, thank you so much."

"Anything for you, love," he said, meaning it.

She turned to look at him, her eyes dancing. "Can we ride now?" she asked, looking so much like an innocent girl asking for a treat that his heart clenched. "Oh, but do we have a side-saddle?" she asked, her face falling comically.

"As if I would give such a gift without thinking of a side-saddle. We've everything you need, and of course we can ride now," he told her, laughing. "Get yourself changed and I'll have her ready for you."

Bea gave a little yip of delight, kissed the mare on the nose and then kissed Justin too, before running back across the stable yard.

"I think she were pleased, my lord," the head groom said wryly as Justin led the mare back to the stall to see to her tack.

"I think so, too," Justin replied with a grin, wondering at how good it made him feel to do something that made Bea happy.

❄ ❄ ❄ ❄ ❄

"Oh, you should see her, Rachel. She's the prettiest creature, and so sweet. Justin says she's got lovely manners, but she's spirited too. He chose her just for me! Isn't that thoughtful of him? For he knows how I have missed riding and—"

"Lord love you, my lady, I can't do these buttons up if you don't hold still," Rachel said in exasperation, as she tried to help Bea into her riding habit at record speed, but Bea could not keep still. She was bursting with excitement, with the joy of a ride on a lovely winter's morning, and the knowledge that Justin had taken such trouble to please her.

The moment she was ready, she ran from the room.

"Don't go breaking your neck!" Rachel called after her, but Bea only laughed, running down the stairs and flying through the front doors so fast Morley stared at her in astonishment.

When she got to the stables, Justin was waiting patiently as he'd promised, with Dove all tacked up and ready with her handsome new side saddle. Bea hurried over to the mounting block and climbed up, smiling delightedly at her husband as he helped her adjust her stirrup and then arranged her heavy skirts neatly. He took a lot of trouble, his hand lingering on her calf, making her aware of the warmth of his palm through her stockings. Finally satisfied, he stood back.

"I like that," he said, gesturing to her new riding habit, which was a vivid blue with black braiding trim. She wore a Glengarry cap of the same colour blue, trimmed with a matching plaited ribbon and a plume of feathers. "I think we must have a painting commissioned of you and Dove together, for I never saw anything so splendid as the two of you."

"Stop!" Bea cried, laughing at him. "If you make me any happier, I shall burst."

Justin grinned at her, looking so genuinely pleased with himself that Bea could not take the smile from her face. She watched as her husband strode over to his own mount, a handsome bay thoroughbred that danced sideways as Justin mounted. Bea's heart skipped as she saw the ease with which he brought the horse under control, his strong thighs flexing in the beautifully tailored breeches that clung to his muscular legs. A surge of excitement thrummed through her, and not only for the coming ride. The sight of her husband astride a horse was one that filled her with pride and a return of the restless impatience that nagged at her with increasing intensity.

"Ready?" Justin asked her.

"Yes," Bea called back, patting Dove's neck before she got the mare trotting out after Justin, following him out of the stable yard.

To begin with, Justin watched her anxiously, obviously concerned in case she had overrated her own skill in the saddle, but after they had been riding for the best part of an hour and taken a couple of jumps she considered extremely tame, he relaxed and gave her an approving nod.

"You ride beautifully, Bea. Your father was quite right to commend you."

Bea flushed with pleasure, delighted by the compliment, but also touched that he'd remembered her comment about her father. "Thank you. Does that mean we can gallop?" she asked hopefully.

Justin laughed and nodded. "There's a big open stretch coming up, love. If you can hold on a few minutes longer," he teased.

Bea stuck her tongue out at him, making him laugh. They carried on, riding through the woodland, the crisp sound of fallen leaves underfoot a soothing backdrop, mingled with birdsong and the occasional huff or whicker from the horses. When they emerged into a large, green field that must be used for grazing, Bea gave an exclamation of delight. They were up high here, stunning views all around, though Bea saw nothing but Justin, his handsome face alight with pleasure as he turned and grinned.

"Ready, love?" he asked, and then galloped away from her.

"Oh! Justin, you devil!" she exclaimed, and charged after him.

Dove flew over the ground, seeming just as joyful as Bea as they galloped after Justin and his mount. Though they had no hope of catching the big thoroughbred, she did not think Dove minded any more than she did. It was simply a moment of pure exhilaration and delight, as everything flew past in a blur and the wind burned Bea's cheeks, making her feel awake and alive in a way nothing else could.

Finally, she slowed Dove, bringing her to a halt beside Justin, who looked just as bright-eyed and energised as she felt. "How was she?"

"Perfection," Bea told him, leaning down to pat the mare's neck. "Absolute perfection."

"Just like her mistress, then," he told her, a gleam in his eyes that made her feel rather reckless.

"Race you back to the house," she suggested, wondering if she was being a fool but not caring.

She took off before he could reply, hearing his shout and ignoring it as she guided Dove back along the ridge, riding flat out, and then cantering as fast as she dared along the paths they had taken to get here. When she got to the stables, she dismounted, jumping nimbly down before a groom could come to help her, and taking a moment to whisper her thanks to Dove and stroke her silken neck. In normal circumstances, she would not have considered leaving her mount in the hands of a groom after a ride, preferring to see to it herself, but as Justin's horse clattered into the yard, she had other things on her mind.

She stared at him for a moment, her lips quirking before she grasped her skirts, calling out to him. "You're not at the house yet!"

With that, she took to her heels and ran, hearing his exclamation as he dismounted. Bea flew along the pathway back to the house, breathless and wishing her corset was not quite so tight. When she got to the front door, she saw Justin was close behind her and gave a little shriek, closing the door on him and sliding the bolt across. She gave a delighted laugh as he pushed at the door.

"Bea! Let me in!" he shouted, though he was laughing too.

Bea stuck her tongue out at him and shook her head. "You lose!" she cried, and ran away, hurrying up the stairs as dignified Morley practically lunged to the front door to open it, looking between the two of them as if they'd run mad.

Perhaps they had, she thought, she had never been happier in her life.

She squealed as Justin pursued her, taking the stairs two at a time. Bea hurried along the corridor, running into her room but not managing to close the door before Justin pushed through it. Gasping, she shrieked as he kicked the door shut and hauled her into his arms.

"Now I have you, wicked creature. What do you mean by running away from your husband?" he mock-scolded her.

"How else could I get you to chase me?" she demanded, and then pressed her mouth to his.

She heard his breath catch, felt the stillness come over him, before he let go and kissed her passionately, devouring her mouth, his tongue tasting and sliding over hers, his breath coming fast.

"Bea," he groaned, dragging his mouth from hers to kiss the line of her jaw, her throat. "Bea, love, I want you. I cannot stop thinking about it, about you."

She smiled at his words, pleased to know he felt such things for her even as a rush of trepidation shivered over her skin. Breathing hard, Justin stopped, resting his forehead against hers.

"Do you want this, Bea? Do you want me?"

Bea hesitated, biting her lip. "I… I think so, yes. Yes," she told him, though her heart hammered in her chest.

"We'll take things slowly," he promised. "Nothing you don't want. If you want me to stop, you say so. If you—"

Bea silenced the words with a kiss. She was too nervous to talk, but she trusted he meant what he said and that was enough.

"Will you lie down with me?" he asked, breaking the kiss and caressing her cheek with his fingers.

Bea nodded, watching as he moved away, sitting on the edge of her bed and pulling off his boots. He stretched out, making it look suddenly small, his large frame dominating the space. Patting the mattress beside him, he smiled.

"Don't be shy, love."

Bea moved to the bed and sat down, looking at Justin. She turned away from him, hiding her blush as she bent and undid the laces on her boots. Still not looking at him, she lay down beside him, staring at the ceiling and feeling suddenly foolish.

"I'm afraid I shan't compare to your lovers," she said in a rush, and then wished she'd said nothing at all.

She felt sick and uncertain when he didn't answer and then started as his warm hand found her cold fingers.

"No, you won't," he said, shocking her momentarily until he carried on. "And I've never been gladder of anything, Bea. I wish I could shed my past like an old coat and leave it behind, but I cannot do that. So, I shall profit from it, because it has taught me to value what I have here with you. It's rare, sweetheart, to be happy in a marriage, to be in love. If I were young and innocent, I might not realise how easy it is to take that for granted. I might not tend to that love with the attention it needs, because I'd be careless with it. I won't be careless with you, Bea, I won't ever take this feeling for granted."

Bea turned to face him, reaching for him as his arms pulled her close and he kissed her, holding her to him. Bea reached up, caressing his face, smiling as her chilly hands made him shiver. He turned her onto her back, and she sighed as some of his weight pressed down on her, though he was careful, holding himself over her as he kissed her, and his hand wandered. Her breath came faster as his palm glided up her side and cupped her breast. Though there were layers of fabric and corset between them, her skin burned where he touched her, the longing to feel his skin against hers sudden and urgent.

She tugged at his neck, pulling him down, kissing him harder, startling a smothered laugh from him that might have been embarrassing if not for the tortured groan that followed. He settled between her legs, the fabric of her riding habit too bulky, too thick, to allow her to feel his body as she longed to do… and then she heard Rachel's voice outside her door, heard her hand on the doorknob.

"Don't come in!" she shouted, and then buried her face in Justin's shoulder, wondering if she would die of mortification.

"Oh… er… right you are," Rachel called uncertainty, followed by the sound of her footsteps hurrying away.

Bea struggled to get up, untangling her skirts from Justin with difficulty.

"S-Sorry," she said, burying her face in her hands.

Lord, what a fool he must think her. But when she looked back, Justin was grinning, his expression wicked.

"I rather like the idea of having an affair with my own wife," he told her, waggling his eyebrows.

She let out a breath, half laughter, half relief. "You're not annoyed?"

"Annoyed?" He looked at her with concern and got to his feet. "Bea, I will wait for you, for as long as you need, and I will never be annoyed."

"Truly?" she pressed as he came around the bed and took her in his arms.

"Truly. Never annoyed," he murmured, nuzzling into her hair and breathing in the scent he found there. "Frustrated, certainly. Filled with longing and desire at every moment of the day and night, but never annoyed, love. Torment me as much as you like. I can take it."

She glanced up at him uncertainly and found nothing but adoration in his eyes.

"I won't torment you," she promised him. "At least, no more than I torment myself."

"That seems fair," he told her, chuckling.

"I… I did want to," she said, embarrassed but needing to explain. "But the idea that Rachel, that the servants knew you were in here, during the day, and—" Bea shook her head in an agony of humiliation.

"I understand," he told her soothingly. "There's not a thing to explain, nor worry about. I promise."

Bea clung to him, resting her head upon his chest. "You are the very best of husbands, Justin."

He stilled at that, and she glanced up, finding him staring at her with a mixture of astonishment and pure delight. "Of all the words I never expected to hear in my life, those had to be at the top of the list." He kissed her forehead. "I will endeavour to remain worthy of them, love. Now, though it pains me, I shall leave you to get changed, before I prove to us both how wrong you are."

He let her go with obvious regret, bent to retrieve his boots, and padded to the door.

"Justin!" she called, when he was halfway out. "Thank you for this morning, for Dove, and… for everything."

To her delight, he blew her a kiss and winked at her before closing the door behind him.

Bea hugged herself tightly, uncertain of what she was feeling aside from pure happiness.

A moment later, there was a knock on the door. "My lady?"

Bea hurried to open it, unable to hide her fiery blush as Rachel came in, giving her a direct look that demanded information.

"Well?" she said, hands on hips. "I hope he was here at your invitation, for if he weren't…"

"Oh, Rachel, yes. Yes, he was," Bea said, sitting at her dressing table and laughing, pressing her palms to her burning cheeks.

"I see," Rachel said, regarding her anxiously. "You think you can trust him, then?"

Bea nodded, staring at Rachel. "I do. I know I can. I cannot explain, Rachel… at least, not all of it, but he's not the devil we thought him."

"My lady," Rachel began, folding her arms and looking sceptical.

"No, Rachel. I don't deny he's got a terrible past, but he says that's why he'll be the model husband. He says he's not young and innocent and careless of the gift he's been given. He says that everything he's done means he knows he must not take what we have for granted but tend it and take care of it. Isn't that lovely?" she said with a sigh.

Rachel blinked, looking rather taken aback. "Well," she said, letting out a breath. "I suppose I owe John an apology."

"You do?" Bea said in surprise.

"He's been telling me since we got here that his lordship is a good man at heart and only needed the right circumstances to bring him around. John said he's kind and loyal, and that he only did the things he did because he was so unhappy. John says you make him happy, my lady."

Bea grinned, feeling elated by the words. "I do," she said, knowing it was true. "He makes me happy too, Rachel. But what else does John say?" she asked, waggling her eyebrows.

Rachel turned an interesting shade of pink and looked flustered.

"Rachel!" Bea said, getting to her feet. "Rachel, you tell me at once. Do I need to have a word with the man or—"

"He's asked me to marry him," Rachel said in a rush, and then clapped a hand to her mouth.

"Oh, Rachel! That's… That's wonderful. Isn't it?" she added, confused by the look on Rachel's face. "Don't you want to marry him?"

"I… I do, my lady, only—"

"Only?"

Rachel sat heavily on the bed and looked up at Bea, her expression beseeching. "Only, I love my job. I was so lucky to get the position as your lady's maid and… and I don't want to give it up."

Bea frowned, moving to sit down beside her and take Rachel's hand. They had never had the formal relationship most ladies had with their maids. Bea had been young when Rachel had come to her and, not having a mother to guide her, she had put her trust in Rachel. She had long ago given up calling her by her last name, even before she had been sent to her uncle's house where she'd been so unhappy. There, Rachel had been her friend and confidante, her ally, and she would never forget that. But it was usual for women to stop working such positions when they married, for the commitments of marriage and children did not sit easily alongside work that took up so much time.

"Well, I don't see why you must. If John accepts it, you will carry on, at least until you have children. I suspect you would wish to stop then, Rachel, but we can figure things out as we go."

Rachel stared at her and then burst into tears. "Oh, my lady. Do you mean it?"

"Well, of course I mean it, you silly goose," Bea said, shaking her head as she hugged Rachel. "Now, stop all this blubbering. You're going to be married! Isn't that wonderful?"

"Yes!" Rachel said, laughing and crying at once now. "Oh, yes, my lady. Yes, it really is."

Chapter 14

"Wherein the delights of married bliss reveal themselves."

28th November 1820.

Justin hummed to himself as he washed and changed for dinner later that same day, looking forward to sharing the evening with his wife. He wondered if Bea would allow him to tumble her onto his lap again and suspected she would. Anticipation thrummed beneath his skin as he wondered what else she might allow him, if he were careful with her. He had meant what he said, he would wait as long as she wanted… but if she *didn't* want, he was equally prepared to encourage her with all the skills at his disposal.

He turned as John held out his waistcoat for him and belatedly realised that his usually loquacious valet was quiet tonight. Shrugging into the waistcoat, he regarded the man who had been a better friend to him than any other he had known and frowned.

"Cat got your tongue, John? Why so troubled? Is aught amiss?"

John went to the bed where he had laid out a coat of bottle-green superfine and stared down at it for a long moment before seeming to come to a decision. "I've asked Rachel to marry me," he said, glancing at Justin to see how this had been taken. "She said yes."

Justin stared at his valet and then gave an exclamation of delight. "Why, John! Congratulations. We must celebrate. This is marvellous news… Isn't it?" he added, regarding John with concern.

"Aye," John said ruefully, grinning at him. "I never reckoned I'd find a lass willing to take me on, let alone one as pretty as Rachel."

"Then why so Friday faced?" Justin demanded with a laugh.

John frowned. "It's just, I wondered… well, Rachel wants to know what will happen when we marry. There's many households that won't allow such things, you see, and so where would we live, and where would I get another job?"

He shrugged miserably as Justin stared with incomprehension.

"What the devil are you blethering on about? Another job? Not let you marry her? John, you're talking to me. *Me!* As if I give a flying fig what anyone else in the *ton* does or does not approve of. Of course you must marry her. Indeed, I insist upon it, for I'll not have such goings on under my roof, my man," Justin said, wagging a disapproving finger at his incredulous valet and rather enjoying himself. "I shall march you up the aisle myself if I must, and what's more, you'll take that handsome cottage on the estate I told you I was furbishing up. Just the thing for a family, I should think, and only a five-minute walk from the house. It's not like I shall need you to pour me into bed at ridiculous hours of the morning any longer. I'm a respectable married man now."

John made a choked sound, and Justin was uncertain if it was shock, amusement, or some other emotion he dared not name, in case it embarrassed them both.

"I hope I've made myself clear, John," Justin said sternly, grinning as his bewildered valet helped him into his coat.

John met his gaze in the looking glass and nodded, his eyes shining. "You have, my lord. Perfectly clear, and I thank you for it. I shall thank her ladyship, too. If you'll forgive me for my impertinence, but the day she turned up on your doorstep was the most fortunate day in both our lives and that's the truth."

"That it was, John," Justin said with a smile. "It certainly was."

❄ ❄ ❄ ❄ ❄

Bea sat at her dressing table, turning the lovely cravat pin she had bought Justin for Christmas back and forth in her hands. She wondered if she could wait until Christmas Day to give it to Justin, for she wanted to see him wear it, to see the devilish glitter in his eyes match the sparkling gem when he was merry and teased her.

"The ribbon you ordered arrived this morning, my lady," Rachel told her, bustling about the room tidying after having dressed Bea for dinner. "There are yards and yards of it. Red and green, and gold too. I can't wait to see the place all prettied up for holidays. Shall we all go and cut greenery like we used to with your pa?"

Bea turned at Rachel's question, focusing on her words, for she had not been paying attention. "Ribbons? Oh, yes, indeed. I shall ask Justin tonight, but I'm sure he will. He enjoyed stirring the pudding and I think he wants to take part in all the Christmas rituals. With the way he was raised, he never had such pleasures and traditions, and I think he delights in discovering them as much as I do in sharing them with him."

"That's good, then," Rachel said, smiling. "John is speaking to him tonight about our future," she added nervously.

"Don't worry, Rachel. It will all be well. Justin won't disappoint you, I promise."

"I hope he don't disappoint you either, my lady," Rachel said with a smile, hesitating with a bundle of petticoats for washing in her arms. "My lady?"

"Yes, Rachel?" Bea said, putting the cravat pin carefully away again.

"I… I hope you don't mind me asking, but what with you having no mama to guide you… Well, do you know what to expect? From the marriage bed, I mean?"

Bea turned on the stool, gazing at Rachel with interest. "A little," she said, frowning. "But… But do *you* know, Rachel?"

Rachel grinned and sat down on the bed, patting the space beside her.

"Come here, my lady, and I'll tell you what you need to know."

❄ ❄ ❄ ❄ ❄

Justin watched his wife with interest as they finished their dinner. She had been in an odd mood this evening. Laughing and merry, but now and then he would catch her looking at him, a speculative gleam in her eyes. When he turned, she would blush and look away. It was most intriguing.

"I've told John that he and Rachel may have the cottage I showed you, the one closest to the house," he told her as he drew out her chair, once the meal was done.

"Oh, Justin. I knew I could rely on you. Rachel was in such a dither, worrying she would have to leave her position, but I told her she need not if she did not wish to. Not until she had a baby, at least. Then we shall have to see, I suppose. You don't mind?"

Justin shook his head. "Of course not. I think we have both been most fortunate in John and Rachel, and I would not diminish their happiness when they have been so good to us."

Bea took his arm and reached up, kissing his cheek fondly and gazing up at him with such admiration he almost blushed. Blushed! *Him!* How extraordinary. Yet she made him feel green and remade in a way he had not thought possible.

"Shall we take a glass of something in your parlour, then?" he asked, looking forward to spending a delightful evening with her in his arms.

She bit her lip, avoiding his gaze, and shook her head. "I'm s-sorry, Justin. I'm rather tired tonight. I think I shall go up. Do you mind?"

"Oh." Disappointment coursed through him, but he smiled and shook his head. "Of course not, love. Though I shall miss you."

"Thank you, Justin," she said demurely, and then fled the room.

Justin frowned, wondering what was wrong with her. Perhaps she had her monthly courses and was feeling under the weather. No doubt she was too embarrassed to mention it. Thinking he would have a drink in his rooms if he must be alone, he made his way back up the stairs to find John waiting for him, which was odd, as he'd not normally be up this early.

Before he could speak, John began going through the nightly ritual, tugging off his boots and pulling his coat from his shoulders.

"John, I'm not going to bed yet," he protested.

"Why not? A good idea. Early night would do you good," John insisted, putting toothpowder on his toothbrush.

Justin threw up his hands and gave in. First Bea, now John. Bewildered but resigned, Justin allowed the man to boss him about until he was finally left alone. Wearing only a heavy satin banyan, he sat by the fire in his bedroom, which John had built up to resemble a small inferno, and stretched out his legs, picking up a book to read. It was one of the novels that Bea had bought and given to him. He was barely three pages in when the door opened quietly.

Justin sighed and lowered the book, expecting to see John again.

"What the devil is wrong with you, man? I assumed you wanted rid of me to spend time with your beloved, but—"

The words died as he turned and saw Bea. She smiled nervously at him as, stunned, he took in the sight of her, her hair unbound and cascading around her shoulders in a curtain of gleaming chestnut locks. Dressed in a delicately embroidered white nightgown, the fabric so fine it looked gauzy and insubstantial, it clung to her delicious curves doing little to hide what lay beneath. She had covered her modesty with a pretty ruffled dressing gown, but as he watched, she allowed it to slide down her arms with a soft sigh of fluttering lace and ribbons.

"Bea," he said stupidly, rooted to the chair.

"Justin," she replied, looking a little pleased with herself at his astonished reaction, as well she might.

"I thought you were tired. I thought—"

"I wanted to surprise you," she replied, moving closer to him. "So I fibbed."

"I *am* surprised," he managed, his voice oddly hoarse. "And delighted."

She grinned at him, looking so adorably smug he could not wait to kiss her.

"Come here," he told her, setting the book aside and holding his arms out to her.

Bea walked to stand before him and he reached for her again, but she pushed his hands away, shaking her head.

Justin watched her cautiously, uncertain now. "You can trust me," he told her, but before he could say more, she gave a huff and shook her head.

"If I didn't think that, I should not be here," she retorted, and then astounded him into speechlessness as she tugged at the delicate ribbon tie of her nightrail and opened the gathered neckline wide, letting it slide down her body to pool in an innocent puddle of white cotton at her feet.

Justin stared, his mouth suddenly dry, his every dream and desire displayed before him.

He got to his feet, tugging her into his arms and revelling in the feel of her warm, silken skin. Justin bent his head and touched his lips to hers. Her mouth was soft and giving and sweet, and desire exploded beneath his skin. Bea pressed closer, her body voluptuous and delicate at once, slender of waist and limb, but plush and plump in all the most interesting places. Justin deepened the kiss, his hands sliding down her back to cup her lovely behind and pull her closer against him. Her breath hitched as she felt the hard pressure of his arousal. He smiled against her mouth as she reached for the tie on his dressing gown, tugging at it with fumbling fingers, only managing to make a knot she could not loosen.

"Take it off," she commanded impatiently.

Justin obeyed, delighted to submit to her every whim. He pushed her eager fingers aside and untied the knot, pulling the heavy satin aside. Her hot gaze drifted down his body, making his blood heat, surging through his veins like liquid paraffin touched by a match.

"Off," she said again, breathless now, pushing the fabric from his shoulders.

"You are dreadfully autocratic," he said mildly, loving that she had taken the situation out of his hands, that taking control of something that made her nervous gave her the courage to see it through.

"I know, but I think you do not mind it. Do you?" There was a note of anxiety there and he smiled, shaking his head.

The desire he saw in her eyes, the need, was enough to make his body rigid with longing, and he shrugged the banyan off, hearing it fall to cover the chair behind him.

"I don't mind in the least," he murmured, his body growing harder still as she stared at him in wonder. "I love it when you are brave, Bea, when you take what you want or need no matter what the world might think of it. So take me, my darling girl, take all of me, the wicked bits and the bits you can be proud of, for they all belong to you now."

She touched the scar on his shoulder with delicate fingers, tracing where he'd been shot during his duel with Lavinia's husband. His breath caught as she pressed a soft kiss to the ugly patch of skin before standing back again and perusing his body once more. Her gaze lingered on the place where his arousal was blatantly obvious, but now she looked up, meeting his eyes. "I want you, Justin. All of you, with no exceptions. Make me yours."

"All in good time, love," he told her, lifting her into his arms and setting her down again in the chair. "There's no rush."

She stared at him in confusion, an almost petulant look of frustration flickering in her eyes. "But Justin, I want you to make love to me. I don't want to just sit here."

"But you will just sit there," he told her sternly, his lips twitching with the desire to smile and kiss the pout from her mouth. "And I shall make love to you."

"Oh," she said, her face clearing. "In a chair? Is that… normal?"

Justin swallowed a bark of laughter, not wanting her to think he was mocking her when he was charmed beyond reason. "What is normal for some is depraved for others, my sweet, so why don't you make up your own mind, as you do about everything else?"

She considered this as he got to his knees, leaning in and pressing a kiss to her mouth, sighing with wonder at the realisation that she was really his, body and soul, as extraordinary as that seemed.

"Very well," she said, sounding decided. She sat back in the chair, staring down at him. "What now?"

"Now, you just sit there and let me do all the work," he told her, smiling helplessly as she burrowed deeper into his heart with every passing second.

She nodded at that, watching him with interest. His hands rested lightly on her knees, and he slid them down her legs to her ankles, lifting her foot to kiss her toes one by one, then the side of her foot, and then the arch beneath.

Bea gave a little squeal and pulled her foot free, giggling. "That tickles!" she protested, shivering. Justin's eyes darkened as he saw the effect this had on her nipples, tightening the delicate pink into tight little buds that made his mouth water.

He grinned at her and dragged her foot back to his mouth, holding it still as she shrieked and squirmed and he laved his tongue between her toes.

"Stop, stop," she said, panting breathlessly.

He chuckled at her theatrics and smiled. "Very well, for now, but one of these days I shall hold you down and tickle you and nothing you can say will make me stop."

She gazed at him, interest sparkling in her eyes, and Justin knew without a doubt she would be a wonderful bed partner, for she was giving and brave and, he thought, not afraid to tell him what she wanted.

For now, he pressed a kiss to her ankle, sliding his hands back up to her knees, kissing her there too as he pushed her legs wide. Her colour rose as he did so, as he pushed his body into the gap and leaned in, sinking his hands into her beautiful hair and kissing her passionately. She met his passion with the full force of her own and he drew back with difficulty, only able to do so for the promise of tasting the delicious breasts that his mouth hungered for.

She gasped as he suckled, her hands holding his head against her, as if she would keep him there always. Not that he minded, her breasts were pillow soft, her skin lightly scented with the delicate perfume of lily of the valley and the uniquely feminine allure of her arousal. Justin pushed her gently back, tugging her legs towards him so she lounged in the chair, her legs splayed out on either side of him as he kissed his way down her body, over the gentle curve of her belly. He lingered to slide his tongue into her belly button for the delight of feeling her squirm beneath him before nuzzling into the dark thatch of springy curls. He glanced up at her then, wondering if her courage would desert her but she gazed back at him, her lips quirking.

"You look just like the fallen angel I once described you as," she murmured, reaching out to tousle his hair fondly. "Wicked as sin, but all mine."

"All yours," he agreed, holding her gaze as he parted her gently and lowered his mouth to cover her feminine heat with his mouth.

Bea gasped, her eyes closing, head falling back against the chair and Justin smiled against her skin as he began his tender torment. He did not allow her a moment of repose, bringing her closer and closer to the peak she struggled for instinctively, before letting it slip from her grasp once more. If there was any good to be found in his decadent skills, he was determined that Bea would profit from them, pleasuring her with mouth and tongue and fingers until her lovely skin was flushed and damp, her eyes glazed with desire, her mind emptied of anything but the feel of his mouth on her, drawing her deeper and deeper into a seductive world she could explore to the fullest, with him as her guide.

When he finally relented, giving her everything she needed to reach the highest heights he could take her to, she shattered, crying out so loud and so long he felt a surge of triumph. His body ached, his arousal throbbing so hard as he watched her come apart, he almost followed her without her ever having laid a hand on him. Justin thought he had never seen anything so erotic, so stirring in his entire life, as the sight of his wife lost to passion.

She came around slowly, her gaze upon him unfocused and languorous as she sighed and stretched like a sleek, sated cat. "You *can* make love in a chair," she said, sounding amused and pleased with herself.

Justin gave a bark of laughter, which sounded a tad desperate even to his ears.

"Come, my love. I need you now," he told her, getting to his feet and tugging her up into his arms. She swayed, too relaxed to stand, so he scooped her up and carried her to the bed. When he laid her down, she only sighed, her limbs arranging themselves in a wanton pose that made his heart thud with mad desire, his entire body poised on a knife's edge. Justin gritted his teeth, telling himself urgently to think boring thoughts.

"You need me?" she whispered, her lovely green eyes focusing hazily on him.

"I do. Desperately. Madly. This moment, love," he told her, his voice trembling as much as his body.

What he needed was evident as he settled between her thighs, his hardness pressing against the part of her that must still be throbbing after his attentions. Bea's eyes widened, staring up at him as a gasp escaped her.

"Will it hurt?" she whispered, suddenly less distracted than she had been.

"Perhaps a little," he said, his voice soothing. "I'll try my best not to, I promise, love. Relax if you can."

"Relax?" she repeated impishly. "With th-that… *there?*"

She snorted irrepressibly, and he laughed, gazing down at her.

"God, I love you, Bea. I love you so much."

She stilled at his words, reaching up to wind her arms around his neck. "I'm so glad, Justin, for I cannot stop loving you now, and I would hate to be the only one so afflicted."

"I have the full measure of this particular torment, but we'll suffer it together, side by side. For always."

"Or one atop the other," she added practically, making him snort this time, shaking his head with amusement. He could not remember ever laughing so with a lover, ever being so ridiculously happy and aroused and giddy with delight.

She closed her eyes and sighed as Justin pressed his mouth to her throat, painting butterfly soft kisses over her skin. He ducked his head again, taking her nipple into his mouth, suckling until she cried out, clinging to him.

"You like that, don't you?" he said, not above feeling a little smug.

"I like all of it," she said, sounding dazed. "But I love you most of all."

Her breath caught and held abruptly as he pressed his arousal more insistently against the seam of her core. Bea's sensitive flesh responded at once, though she still jolted in shock as he sought entry. Justin soothed her, kissing her deeply, caressing her body, easing his way inside with ever-increasing pushes and slight retreats that had her panting with a combination of pleasure and pain.

"Oh, God, Bea," he groaned, out of his mind with the perfection of it, the feel of her feminine heat welcoming him inside. "So… So lovely…"

She tensed as he pushed on, and Justin groaned as he found he was fully inside her. He stilled, allowing her body to accept him. Bea breathed hard and steady, clutching at his shoulders. He felt her palms gliding over his hot skin, moving down his back to grasp his buttocks and Justin smiled inwardly as she kneaded and clung to him. He moved, sliding back and thrusting home again.

"Oh!" she cried. Bea's eyes flew open as he retreated and pushed forward again, gently at first and then with increasing speed and force, as he loved her with all the skill and passion at his disposal.

"Justin!" she cried breathlessly, and he moaned, the guttural sound clearly pleasing her for her body reacted, squeezing around him.

"Oh, love," he said, his voice ragged, groaning as she did it again, deliberately this time. He wondered at his own lack of control, at the difference there was between bedding a woman he desired but did not love, and making love to his wife, the woman who held his heart. It was as if music had been described to him and he understood what it was, but he'd never heard it himself before, but now it rang in his ears with such beauty he was overwhelmed by it.

"Don't…" he managed desperately. "I can't if you… Oh, Christ, Bea."

He kissed her and Bea wrapped herself around him, clinging to him like she would never let him go. *Don't let me,* he thought, holding her to him. *Don't ever let me go.*

"I love you," he said, needing to imprint the words on her mind, on the memory of this moment forever. "I love you. I need… always, Bea, for always…"

His body shuddered and jerked, and he uttered a coarse exclamation that he feared might shock her, but she just clung harder. Her body pulsed around him, squeezing and grasping at him, sending him higher than even he'd thought possible, as she held on tight and called his name, and the world fell away.

Epilogue

"Wherein even the most jaded heroes get a merry Christmas, and a happy ever after."

24th December 1820.

Bea stood back, regarding the mantelpiece in her parlour with approval. They had all gone out early that morning, gathering greenery to decorate the house. From butler and valet to the lowliest scullery maid, Bea had insisted that everyone should take part and have a chance to decorate the house. She had arranged a cold meal with Mrs Kershaw to ensure the workload was lightened and, upon their return, the entire staff had been treated to a cup of mulled wine and mince pies with the master and mistress as they gathered in the hallway to sing Christmas carols.

Ever since, the house had been a hive of activity and rang with laughter and the sound of carols being sung or whistled, either well or entirely off key.

"You've outdone yourself, I reckon," Rachel said with approval, admiring the display of holly, ivy, and fir. It was decorated with clove-studded oranges, cinnamon sticks, red apples and fir cones, and red and gold ribbons. The scent of spice and greenery wafted up as the fire warmed the pretty bough and Bea hugged her arms about herself, nodding.

"I think you are right, Rachel. It looks splendid. The entire house looks splendid, though, and I could not have done it without you and John."

Rachel snorted and waved this comment away.

"Ah, there you are," Justin said, pushing into the room and grinning as he held a bunch of mistletoe aloft. "Fair game, both of you, I reckon."

He made a leering face at Rachel, who shrieked and ran from the room, laughing.

"Well, that's got rid of her," he said with satisfaction. "Now, for my real prey."

He lunged for Bea, who didn't move an inch.

"You're supposed to scream and flee," he told her impatiently. "How can I catch you and ravish you if you don't run away?"

"But I don't want to run away," she replied, putting her arms around his neck. "So, you'll just have to ravish me here."

Justin sighed and tossed the mistletoe over his shoulder. "My efforts are wasted on you," he grumbled, but kissed her deeply and passionately and looked rather pleased with himself when he let her up.

Bea sighed happily and rested her head on his chest.

"Lovely," she said happily.

Justin snorted. "Did I see Morley hand you a letter earlier?"

"Oh! I almost forgot," Bea said, raising her head. "Yes, it came from France. Lavinia. She's found her comte, and he still wants her. They're to be married in Paris… well, they must *be* married by now. She said before Christmas. Isn't that splendid? Now her baby is safe, and she has the man she wished to marry before her parents interfered."

"All's well that ends well," he murmured, gazing down at her.

"Thanks to you for arranging her passport for her and getting her to France," she told him, distractedly rearranging the folds of his cravat.

"Stop that," he scolded. "John gets tetchy if you muss up his work."

She pulled a face at him and then fidgeted.

"What?" he asked, knowing by now that she was impatient about something.

"It's no good. I can't do it. I don't want to wait for tomorrow," she said, and hurried from the room.

"What—" Justin began and then followed her out. "Bea?" he called, but she was running up the stairs.

"Stay there," she told him. "Don't move."

Justin turned to see John and Rachel watching him with amusement and threw up his hands. "She's run mad," he said with a shrug.

"Your fault," John replied, shaking his head. "Happens to the best of us."

"John," Rachel exclaimed, giving her new husband a look of outrage at him speaking so boldly to his master.

John just shrugged but Rachel took pity on him. "She's gone to get your Christmas present, my lord," she said in an undertone. "She's been that impatient to give it to you, I wonder she's waited this long."

"My Christmas present?" Justin replied, delighted by this information. "Well, that means I don't have to wait for tomorrow, either. John, is everything—?"

"Aye, my lord," John said, nodding. "It nearly broke mine and three of the footmen's backs finishing what you started, but it's all ready."

"Excellent," Justin said, beaming at them and rubbing his hands. He went back into the parlour and stood by the fire, waiting for his wife to reappear.

She did a moment later, and he could not help but admire her. Her glossy chestnut hair was arranged beautifully, and she wore a deep red gown chosen for its festive colour. His heart gave an uneven thud at the delighted smile she gave him as she closed the door and ran to him.

"Here!" she said, holding out a small rectangular box. "Merry Christmas, Justin."

Justin stared at her for a moment before leaned in and kissed her. "Thank you," he said, his tone serious.

She laughed and gave him a little push. "You've not opened it yet!" she protested.

"I don't care. I've never had a proper Christmas before, not with decorations and carols and all the festive cheer. I'm thanking you for that, Bea, and for giving me the chance to be a better man than I have been."

"Oh, Justin, don't make me cry," she admonished him, but reached up on her toes and kissed him hard. Breaking the kiss, she flapped her hands at him. "Now open it!"

Justin laughed and unwrapped the pretty parcel, untying the green ribbon with care. He opened the box to discover an elegant gold cravat pin with a large, dark blue sapphire sparkling in the gold setting.

"Oh, I was right," she crowed, looking pleased with herself. "It's the exact same colour as your eyes. Here, let me."

Justin found words failed him, so he stood, docile, as his wife removed the jade pin he had chosen that morning and replaced it with the sapphire. Bea tweaked his cravat, settling the stone to her satisfaction before she stood back to admire her work.

"It's perfect. I knew it would be. It sparkles just like your eyes do when you say something wicked."

He grinned at that and pulled her back into his arms. "If I'd known how much you enjoy me saying wicked things to you, I'd have taken advantage of it," he murmured against her neck, kissing it and brushing his mouth down to her collarbone.

Bea laughed. "Well, you know it now."

Justin raised his head, smiling at her. "I do," he said. "And I shall scandalise you terribly when I take you to bed tonight, my sweet Beatrice. However, if you are allowed to give Christmas presents early, then so am I. Come."

He took her by the hand and hurried from the room.

"Where are we going? What is it?" Bea demanded, her face alight with excitement.

"You'll see in a moment," he told her, pressing a finger to his lips and refusing to say more.

"Well, it can't possibly be as wonderful as Dove, but whatever it is, I shall love it. You give the most delightful presents, Justin," she said as he guided her to the library and opened the door.

She had overseen the renovation of this room, and the handsome oak shelves had all been repaired and polished to a high shine, awaiting their books. The walls were painted a dark green, and the windows had been hung with heavy damask curtains. Comfortable leather chairs and a deep sofa adorned with plump velvet cushions were arranged around the massive fireplace where a fire crackled. It was the perfect place to curl up with a good book… the only thing missing.

In the centre of the room were dozens of huge packing crates. They had not been there the last time Bea had entered the room, for Justin, John, and three of the footmen had hauled the massive things in last night, while Bea was taking her bath. Justin could not remain to finish the job entirely as he needed to be ready for dinner with Bea, but John had done sterling work in bringing the last crates in.

She turned to him in surprise, pointing at the crates.

"What are all those?"

"A bookshop, love," he told her, grinning broadly. "I feared you might one day get lost in a bookshop and never leave, remember? So, I bought the entire contents of the shop in the Pantiles for you. It won't fill the library entirely, I fear, but it's an excellent start."

"Oh!" Bea said, covering her hands with her mouth.

"Now, if I can't find you, I shall know where to look," he said, standing behind her and sliding his arms around her waist. "Do you like it, Bea?"

She turned in his embrace and threw her arms about his neck. "I love it, and I love you, Justin. What a splendid present. You've made me so very happy. Not just with this, but… but everything. I'm so glad you're mine, my own wicked rogue."

Justin grinned at her, having no complaint to make about that. He was quite content to continue to be just a little bit wicked, with his wife in his arms… though now, any licentious behaviour would be exclusively for her.

Wishing you a Merry Christmas,

From,

Emma V Leech

For more Holiday tales in the Rogues & Gentlemen series...

A Rogues and Gentlemen Christmas

A Compilation of Christmas Novellas
Rogues and Gentlemen

A Compilation of THREE Christmas tales from the Rogues & Gentlemen Series...

****

<u>Winter's Wild Melody/</u>

Caught in the storm on his way home after a week of overindulgence, Viscount Debdon takes shelter in an abandoned farmhouse, only to realise...

He is not alone.

When his ghostly companion is revealed to be not only an earthly body, but a heavenly one too, the temptation to remain lost in the woods is hard to resist.

****

The Christmas Rose

The youngest son of a marquess ...

Darkly handsome Ludo - universally known as Lascivious Lord Courtney - is the wickedest rake in Christendom. With a reputation that makes nice young ladies swoon, he is just not the marrying kind.

A friend to the rescue...

Unwitting wallflower Felicity Bunting is only trying to protect a friend when she finds herself in a compromising position with this lusty lord.

An unlikely pairing.

\She might not have meant to do it, but Bunty just accidentally trapped Lord Courtney into marriage.

Neither of them is what the other ever expected to have, but perhaps they might be all they ever wanted.

****

The Winter Bride

Widowed farmer Ned Hardy is facing a bleak winter and a lonely Christmas, when a beautiful young woman turns up on his doorstep in the middle of the night, frozen and terrified.

Stunned by the arrival of a fine lady who looks like a Christmas angel, all of Ned's protective instincts flare to life.

Grace Honeyfield is on the run from her abusive brother and the terrifying man he's forcing her to marry. Escaping into the darkness on a snowy night, she stumbles onto an isolated farm, and into the arms of a handsome farmer. Although not a gentleman by birth, Grace comes to realise Ned deserves the title more than any well-bred man of her acquaintance.

When Ned offers to marry Grace to keep her safe, he dares hope that the future might hold more happiness than the past. To his astonishment, Grace agrees to his proposal, and Ned can't help but wonder if all his Christmases have come at once.

Free to read with your Kindle Unlimited

Get your copy here: A Rogues and Gentlemen Christmas

And for even more Holiday fun…

The Girl is Not for Christmas

A Christmas Regency Romance Novel

After a series of disastrous investments, her family is on the brink of bankruptcy. Now, Olivia is the only thing standing between her brother Charlie's rapidly growing family and penury. Olivia has one chance to capture the eye of a wealthy man and marry well. Her great aunt's lavish New Year ball. Between now and then, Livvy must transform herself from who she is, into a woman who can drive a respectable fellow mad with desire. An impossible task.

Ever practical, she knows there is only one man who can help with her transformation –

The notorious Earl of Kingston, dubbed the King of Sin by the scandal sheets, is recovering from the toll taken by his immoral lifestyle. With his own financial and private affairs in a mess, King escapes London to stay with his old friend Charlie for Christmas.

When his friend's odd little sister demands his helps to learn the art of seduction, King is at once horrified, intrigued, and too bloody wicked to refuse.

Before the holiday is over, King is in way over his head and must persuade Livvy that the King of Sin is dead, and he's the man she needs.

Free to read with Kindle Unlimited

Get your copy here:

The Girl is not for Christmas

Now, from the author of Rogues & Gentlemen, Girls Who Dare, Daring Daughters, and Wicked Sons, comes a brand new series.

When a quiet English seaside village is swept into the glittering world of Regency high society, everything changes.

Suddenly, the once-peaceful shores are teeming with scandalous rakes, battle-weary soldiers seeking redemption, and the crème de la crème of the ton—all desperate for a fresh start and a taste of forbidden romance.

Enter the world of The Venturesome Ladies of Little Valentine.

Cupid Comes to Little Valentine

The Venturesome Ladies of Little Valentine, Book 1

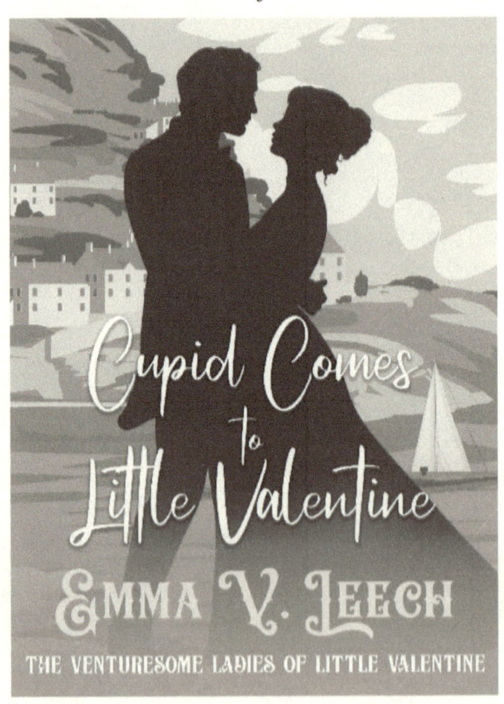

Sylvester Cavendish, the Earl of Beaumarsh, is idle, vain, and utterly unsuited to the sleepy seaside town of Little Valentine. He's only there because his loyal valet, Kirby, has whisked him away after a failed attempt on Beau's life—an attempt orchestrated by his own cousin, Cuthbert, who is impatient to inherit the earldom. Little Valentine, beloved by retirees and the elderly for its tranquil waters, is the last place Beau would ever choose for refuge.

Still suffering from his cousin's poison, Beau's arrival is anything but discreet. He makes a memorable entrance by being sick on the shoes of Miss Clementine Honeywell, the capable and quick-witted daughter of the local vicar.

Clementine is unimpressed by the notorious earl's reputation—and even less impressed by his refusal to confront his murderous cousin. frustrated by Beau's indolence, Clementine takes matters into her own hands, determined to vanquish the villain herself.

But as she faces danger head-on, Clementine discovers there's more to Beau than meets the eye—and perhaps, beneath his idle exterior, a heart worth saving.

Order your copy here: Cupid Comes to Little Valentine

And coming soon, the next novel in the Wicked Sons Series

A Wicked Business

Wicked Sons, Book10

The story of Mr. Felix Knight and Lady Belinda Madox-Brown…. More to be revealed.

Pre-order yours here:

A Wicked Business

About Me!

I started this incredible journey way back in 2010 with The Key to Erebus but didn't summon the courage to hit publish until October 2012. For anyone who's done it, you'll know publishing your first title is a terribly scary thing! I still get butterflies on the morning a new title releases, but the terror has subsided at least. Now I just live in dread of the day my daughters are old enough to read them.

The horror! (On both sides I suspect.)

2017 marked the year that I made my first foray into Historical Romance and the world of the Regency Romance, and my word what a year! I was delighted by the response to this series and can't wait to add more titles. Paranormal Romance readers need not despair, however, as there is much more to come there too. Writing has become an addiction and as soon as one book is over, I'm hugely excited to start the next so you can expect plenty more in the future.

As many of my works reflect, I am greatly influenced by the beautiful French countryside in which I live. I've been here in the Southwest since 1998, though I was born and raised in England. My three gorgeous girls are all bilingual and my husband Pat, myself, and our four cats consider ourselves very fortunate to have made such a lovely place our home.

KEEP READING TO DISCOVER MY OTHER BOOKS!

Other Works by Emma V. Leech

Rogues & Gentlemen

Rogues & Gentlemen Series

The Venturesome Ladies of Little Valentine

The Venturesome Ladies of Little Valentine

Girls Who Dare

Girls Who Dare Series

Daring Daughters

Daring Daughters Series

Wicked Sons

Wicked Sons Series

The Regency Romance Mysteries

The Regency Romance Mysteries Series

The French Vampire Legend

<u>The French Vampire Legend Series</u>

<u>The French Fae Legend</u>

<u>The French Fae Legend Series</u>

<u>Stand Alone</u>

<u>The Book Lover</u> (a paranormal novella)
<u>The Girl is Not for Christmas</u> (Regency Romance)

Audio Books

Don't have time to read but still need your romance fix? The wait is over…

By popular demand, get many of your favourite Emma V Leech Regency Romance books on audio as performed by the incomparable Philip Battley and Gerard Marzilli. Several titles available and more added each month!

Find them at your favourite audiobook retailer!

Acknowledgements

Thanks, of course, to my wonderful editor Kezia Cole with Magpie Literary Services

To Victoria Cooper for all your hard work, amazing artwork and above all your unending patience!!! Thank you so much. You are amazing!

To my BFF, PA, personal cheerleader and bringer of chocolate, Varsi Appel, for moral support, confidence boosting and for reading my work more times than I have. I love you loads!

A huge thank you to all of my beta readers and cheering section! You guys are the best!

I'm always so happy to hear from you so do email or message me :)

emmavleech@orange.fr

To my husband Pat and my family ... For always being proud of me.

Want more Emma?

If you enjoyed this book, please support this indie author and take a moment to leave a few words in a review. *Thank you!*

To be kept informed of special offers and free deals (which I do regularly) follow me on *https://www.bookbub.com/authors/emma-v-leech*

To find out more and to get news and sneak peeks of the first chapter of upcoming works, go to my website and sign up for the newsletter.
http://www.emmavleech.com/

Or follow me here......

http://viewauthor.at/EmmaVLeechAmazon